The Angel in the Mirror
The City Under Seattle

Thea Thomas
&
Blythe Ayne

The Angel in the Mirror
The City Under Seattle

by

Thea Thomas

The Angel in the Mirror
Thea Thomas & Blythe Ayne

Emerson & Tilman, Publishers
129 Pendleton Way #55
Washougal, WA 98671

The Angel in the Mirror

Copyright © Emerson & Tilman
Cover Image of Nikki by Paul Winter
Thea@EmersonandTilman.com
Blythe@BlytheAyne.com

ebook ISBN: 978-1-947151-93-2
Paperback ISBN: 978-1-947151-94-9
Hardbound ISBN: 978-1-957272-33-7
Large Print ISBN: 978-1-957272-34-4
Audiobook ISBN: 978-1-957272-35-1

[1. YOUNG ADULT FICTION/Paranormal, Occult & Supernatural
2. YOUNG ADULT FICTION/Romance/Contemporary
3. FICTION/Fantasy/Urban] I. Title.
BIC: FM

DEDICATION

To All Who Believe in Angels

Books by Thea Thomas

Contemporary Sweet Romance:
Canyon Road
One Love
Two Weddings
Three Proposals

Books by Thea Thomas &
Blythe Ayne
Young Adult:
The People in the Mirror
Millie in the Mirror
The Angel in the Mirror

Paranormal Romance:
Amethyst Dream
Porcelain Claws

Table of Contents

Chapter 1

Mysterious Library

Yumi and I sat cozily at the little kitchen nook table. I was waiting for a call from Mitch, who was getting his old Chevy a much-needed tune-up. As soon as he got back, the plan was he'd pick up Alex, then call me and Yumi, and we'd scurry down to the front door. Off we'd go for a day's exploration of the underground city.

Right then my phone pinged. I was surprised to see it wasn't Mitch. It was Dad. "Good morning my little hummingbird. How's it going?"

"Going great, Dad. What's up?"

"Well, I'm just sitting here in the O.C. airport waiting to go to a meeting in Victoria, B.C., which isn't until tomorrow. And then it dawned on me, as I have a connection in Seattle, I could take a later flight and you could come to the airport and we could have lunch together!" His tone had risen half-an-octave in his enthusiasm.

My eyebrows went straight up into my bangs. "Lunch at SeaTac *today?*"

Yumi's shocked expression matched mine.

"Sure! Spontaneous fun, right?"

"Ahm. But, Dad … I'd love to see you and all, but not only will it take me as long to get to the airport—*spontaneously*—as it will take you to get there from Orange County ... I … I have plans for the day."

There was a pause. "You can't change your plans for your dear old dad?"

I felt like a criminal, hearing his hurt tone of voice. "I *could*, Dad. But it's not just my plans, it's three other people's plans, too. And, again, I'd have to get to the airport …."

"Right. Oh, of course, other people's plans. And getting to the airport." He paused again. "I didn't really think it through, did I?" His voice sounded a bit more chipper. "Well, you know, your dad means well, even when he misfires."

I started feeling unpleasantly, darkly worse. I'm an ogre, I'm a terrible person. Would it truly be so impossible to change everyone's plans and get to the airport? I started to waffle when Mitch's call came in. "Hang on a sec, Dad. Mitch is calling."

"That's okay, sweetie. I'll ring off now. Have a great day." He hung up.

I connected with Mitch.

"Ready to go? We're out front."

"Ah, right. We'll be right down." I clicked off.

"You should see your face, Nikki," Yumi said.

"I'm a terrible person." I got up and headed for my bedroom to get my backpack. "A terrible, terrible person," I muttered down the hall.

I stepped into my closet to grab a jacket, and right then, the mirror started stirring and roiling.

"*Now?*" I whispered, wanting, rather, to yell. "You're going to demand my attention *right now?* Don't I have enough to deal with?"

But I couldn't not watch, and as I did, the sepia stirring started to take shape—a large, high-ceilinged room, dark walnut wainscoting, and rows of long walnut tables, with little dark green lights on them, with accompanying walnut chairs neatly lined up at the tables.

Except for one chair, where a man sat hunched over a huge book or newspaper—I couldn't quite make it out.

"It's a library," I said softly.

But—*why was I seeing this?* Who was this man?

As if in response to my thought, the vision slowly moved around to his side. I couldn't believe it. It looked like—*it looked like Homer*, our beloved doorman.

What could that mean?

"Are you coming, Nikki?" Yumi asked, coming into my room. "They're waiting for us. I just got a call from Alex."

The vision quickly faded. "Yeah. Sorry. Couldn't find my jacket," I white-lied, coming out of my closet, jacket in hand. "Let's … go."

Yumi gave me a really hard look. "You look … strange."

"I *am* strange! Come on!"

I grabbed my backpack and we hurried down to the front door, where Homer, all smiles as always, held the door open for us. "Your carriage awaits, young ladies!"

"Thank you, Homer," we said in unison.

But I couldn't help giving him a studied glance. Why-oh-why had he just appeared in a vision in my scrying mirror?

As we hurried out to the car, Alex jumped out of the front seat, and opened the back door, while Yumi got in the back and I joined Mitch in the front. Doors clanged shut and we all waved to Homer as we took off.

"Got the old jalopy tuned tie-up and ready for more adventure," Mitch said, as he made his way into the traffic.

"Right," I said softly.

He glanced over at me. "What's …."

"She's feeling terrible because her dad just called and said he'd be at SeaTac this afternoon on his way to Victoria, and she should come out to the airport and have lunch with him," Yumi offered from the back seat. "She told him she had plans."

"I'm a terrible person," I reiterated.

"Oh, Nikki! You should have lunch with your dad," Mitch said. "We can explore any time."

"Well, yes. But, spontaneously like that, I couldn't see changing everyone's plans, just because he couldn't plan a bit himself. If Mom had been with him she would have put a stop to it before his phone finished dialing my number. He didn't mean it bad. But it's as if I'm a house plant, sitting on a shelf, waiting for his sunshine, or something."

"Ah! Guilt brings out the poet in you."

"*Hmmmm.*" I looked out the side window at the storefronts passing by, thinking about how much I'd been looking forward to this very day, just to have some fun and not have to take care of anything, the four of us exploring the underground city.

I'd gone through a lot the last few days—helping Yumi's mother tie up her business of turning the gold antique coins into modern-day cash, then getting her to the airport.

And, *finally*, making the adjustment back home, with just Yumi and me there—at last!

The view out the window began to shift to fewer houses and more open terrain. I sighed deeply.

This is what I needed! Some open space, some sunshine, and some silly no-agenda banter with my best friends.

But Dad! I hadn't seen him in weeks, and it was so sweet that he wanted to spend time with me. Not every girl had a father who doted on her. My own best friend in the back seat hadn't had her father in her life since she was five.

Urg! All that, and *furthermore!* I had to contemplate the vision of Homer in the mirror. There was too much to think about. Would it be asking too much to simply let my brain be empty for a while? I wanted not to have to think about anything. I needed a white-noise-mind-noise-cancelling space.

The terrain around us had become even more open with more green rolling hills than houses. The sunlight and green vista let me release my anxiety and circling thoughts yet more, and I sighed deeply.

"Goodness!" Mitch said. "You let go of something!"

"*Oh! Sorry!*" I smiled at him, sheepishly.

"Nothing to apologize for! You've had a lot to deal with, and now your Dad adds to it. I think it all merits several large sighs."

"Probably. But I think I'll reserve the others for later," I giggled. We pulled onto the grassy hillside under which the Victorian underground Seattle lay sleeping. "Oh, boy, here we are!" I exclaimed.

We piled out and gathered our flashlights and backpacks. Mitch led the way down the dirt steps into the bowels of the earth. But we all paused on the four steps around the antique poster of Millie the Milliner, silently paying a few moments of homage to Yumi's several-Greats Aunt, who had reached out from the past and saved her great-great, darling, nieces.

Then we continued down into the darkness-of-darkness, which always, strangely, became so much lighter, once we'd been there for a while.

When we were all on the boardwalk, Mitch asked, "Do we want to explore a house we haven't gone into yet, or do we want to continue farther than we've gone before?"

"I'd kinda like to see the inside of the houses near Aunt Meechie's," Yumi said.

Both Mitch and Alex made vague noises in agreement.

But I felt something well up in me that I could not stop. "I want to continue on. I … I feel like I really have to see something further on." *Wow!* Where was this coming from? I mean, why did I care? I just wanted to hang out with my friends. Any exploration we did should be fine with me. But it wasn't.

"Well, that's okay too," Yumi said in her soft, sweet voice. "The houses are probably not going anywhere. We can explore them some other time."

It was dark, but I could feel them all looking at me like, "What's up with Nikki?"

"Sorry." There I was, apologizing again! "I just … just sort of feel like there's something I'll see that I … need to see."

"Let's do it!" Alex said diplomatically.

I have the best friends in the whole entire world! Every one of them takes my weirdness in stride.

Off we went into the darkness, our flashlights weaving a path on the boardwalk, with Mitch leading the way. Even though we could walk two abreast, we'd agreed to walk single file, just in case we encountered anything unanticipated—like the boardwalk suddenly gone, or whatever.

We made fairly quick progress along the path we were familiar with, but before long, we found ourselves in new territory. Or at least it was for Alex and Yumi.

"Oh, look at that house. I haven't seen it before," Yumi exclaimed.

"Me neither," Alex said, as we stopped before a particularly large, ornate, Victorian house.

"I've seen it," I said, remembering the time I went looking for Mitch when we were in the throes of sorting out our relationship. Goodness, that seemed like a long, *long* time ago!

"Oh, right. That night," Mitch said softly.

"That night," I nodded. He and I exchanged a look. Our relationship had grown to a whole new level that night. "Let's continue," I urged. There was something I *had* to see. I didn't know what it was, but it called to me, just the same.

So we continued on, saying little, cautioning one another to be careful when the boardwalk became a bit wobbly for a span. But then it felt sturdy underfoot again.

Now we'd gone farther than I'd ever been, and it had become ever darker. I could barely see Mitch's shoes in front of me. "Have you been this far before?" I asked him.

"Yes, and farther still. There's a 'Y' up ahead on the path."

We fell into a silent lock-step, and sure enough, before long, the boardwalk came to a 'Y.'

We stood in a tight bunch at the 'Y,' flashlights playing on the walls around us.

> *Two roads diverged in a wood, and I –*
> *I took the one less traveled by"*

Alex quoted.

"Beautiful," Yumi whispered.

"Very beautiful," I agreed. "But I'm pretty sure *both* of these roads have been 'much less traveled by' for a very, very, long time. Not counting Mitch, of course. Which path did you take? We'll go the other way so it's new for you, too."

"I went right," he gestured with his flashlight.

"Left it is!" I said.

Mitch turned and led the way down a road that,
I felt certain, would make all the difference....

10 - The Angel in the Mirror

Chapter II
Victorian Mercantile

We'd gone about a city block further when the residential houses stopped, and we came alongside a building that had written on the front in well-preserved, light-colored letters, "Seattle Mercantile."

"Wow! That could be pretty interesting," Alex exclaimed.

Everyone agreed, including me. But, still, no. I had an unrest, a sense that I must see *something*—I didn't know what—but I would know it when I saw it. "Let's check it out on the way back."

"Okay," Alex said reluctantly.

"How much farther do you want to go?" Mitch asked.

"I don't know. I just … know I'll know it when I see it."

"Oh! You're looking for something specific?"

"I … I don't know," I stuttered. "I sort of think so. At least, I have a feeling. Let's just continue."

And so on we went, everyone humoring me. I really have to stop this princess routine, I tried to tell myself. But I was not about to listen. However, it was not long before we encountered the decision being made for me. We came upon a locked gate, in the middle of the boardwalk.

"That's strange," Mitch reached out and rattled the handle. It was shut and locked tight.

"For sure," I agreed. "What sense does it make to have a locked gate on a public boardwalk?"

It was a beautifully ornate, black wrought iron, seven-foot-tall, locked, arched gate, with a classic Victorian fence leading down from the gate on either side. "Strange, but intentional. What's on the other side?"

We turned our lights to the other side of the gate and fence. A formidable building came into sketchy view up a slight incline as our paltry little lights played around on its surface.

"What is it?"

Mitch's light found a bronze sign not ten feet from us. *"SEATTLE LIBRARY"* was blazoned on it in ornate, but very readable letters.

"Now *THAT* would be interesting," Alex declared.

"Yes. It would," I agreed.

"Is it a hit?" Yumi asked. "Is this what you've been looking for?"

"I believe it's a hit," I said softly, nodding.

"Well, it may be a hit, but we aren't going there without some tools to get through this beautiful but locked gate. It's so beautiful, I don't want to deface it." Mitch rattled the handle again. "But that may be our only option."

We all trained our lights on the *"SEATTLE LIBRARY"* sign, and I suddenly felt chills run right through me. I shivered.

"Cold?" Mitch asked, putting his arm around me.

"Not exactly. Something just … ran through me."

"Yikes!" Alex whispered.

"Not bad, I don't think. But just … something …." No, I wouldn't mention Homer right now. Mostly because I didn't know what I'd say—"I saw Homer in this library this morning in my mirror"? Well, that seemed impossible, and I didn't even know if it was true.

I'd just have to wait until the strange new mystery swirling around Homer and—*maybe*—this library, got some clarity. I turned around on the boardwalk. "Let's check out that mercantile."

"Let's!" Yumi agreed, turning to lead the way back along the boardwalk to the store.

When we came to it, we stopped in our little huddle and trained our lights up to the store's front door. Silently, we watched, with our lights on the charming stone path that led to the front door as Mitch cautiously went ahead of us and stepped up onto the porch of the mercantile, then, seeing all was safe, we followed him.

Big windows with small panes of glass lined the front of the store. I could see the shadowy forms of manikins in Victorian clothing, along with numerous other objects that I could not make out.

Mitch turned the door handle. *"Ohhhh!"* we all exclaimed as the door opened with a long, loud, protesting *creaaaaak!*

But! It *did* open! One-by-one, we stepped inside, flashing our lights around upon the world of over a century before, encapsulated before our eyes. Tools, bolts of fabric, pots, and pans, and giant bins marked "flour," "sugar," "salt," and even "baking soda" surrounded us. There were books on a shelf above a row of gorgeous fountain pens along with a neat row of pencils, "Seattle Mercantile" stamped on them.

"Don't touch anything," Yumi warned, "remember how that gorgeous purple hat in my Aunt's millinery completely disintegrated when I barely touched it."

"Right," I agreed, although I longed to take a peek inside a few of the books with titles I'd never heard of.

"The tools are touchable," Alex said, holding up some strange metal object.

"What is that?" I asked.

"I don't know, but I'm sure it was very good at doing whatever its mysterious job was!" Alex joked.

"Oh, Nikki, come and look at this beautiful silver!" Yumi stood over a showcase, shining her light down into it. I joined her.

"Wow!" In the glass case I saw an array of delicate, embossed sterling silver items, also as completely mysterious as to their possible

function as the strange tool Alex held. But, still, so beautiful!

Yumi carefully slid open the case and picked one of the items up. "Hold your light here, Nikki, so I can read the description."

I held my light on the small note in the showcase. "Strawberry picker," Yumi read. She put her thumb and middle finger into the silver loops of the beautiful little device. "Oh! I see. So everyone wouldn't have their grubby fingers on the strawberries. My goodness, they thought of everything!"

"And made it beautiful, too!" I stepped over to the next showcase. "Oh, Yumi, look at these chatelaine—beautiful! A little notepad, a little pen, scissors, and … other things on these ornate silver chains."

"Ohhh … I need something like that for my art—wouldn't it be inspiring to wear that charming little pencil and sketch pad?"

I thought, well, you and your mom own this land now—that chatelaine *is* yours. But I didn't say anything, as so many other thoughts raced through my mind at the same time. Would we really want to change anything here, while on another hand, these things ought to be getting used, especially that beautiful pen and notepad by my extremely talented friend.

"I guess …." Yumi said hesitantly, "I guess my mom and I sort of own it, don't we?"

I nodded but kept silent.

"Well, I don't want to change anything here. But I like the concept. I need to come up with something like it on my own."

"You could!" I suddenly noticed that Mitch was no longer with us. I turned in a complete circle, looking for him. "Where's Mitch?"

Alex looked around. "I don't know!"

Yumi and I joined Alex. Standing in a tight knot, we flashed our lights flashing around the shop and out through the front windows, with the lights reflecting back at us on the glass.

But no Mitch. I moved to the back of the store where I saw a door standing partially ajar. Cautiously, I stepped into the dark space, my two friends behind me. There were shovels and pitchforks and other large tools hanging from the walls and leaning up against one another. Things hung down from the dark ceiling, their indistinct shapes making everything even spookier.

I came to another door, also slightly open, and stopped. "Mitch? Are you in here?"

"Yes, Nikki, I'm here. Come and see this."

I followed his voice, stepping through the door into a hallway, then passing into another room. Mitch stood with his flashlight trained overhead on a face—a beautiful face, but still, I let out a small "*eek!*" and just about fainted.

He stood before a ten-foot-tall, white marble angel, wings outspread almost to the extent of the room. Mitch came over to me and put his arm around me. "Sorry! I didn't think about the effect it might have on you. I should have said something."

With my heart still pounding from the startling sight, I leaned into him. "Amazing! So beautiful. Goodness, how did they even get it in here?"

"*Ohhh!*" Yumi cried, coming into the room, in tandem with Alex's "*Whoa!*"

"And why didn't you react like we all did, with some exclamation?"

Mitch chuckled. "I think I was simply too overwhelmed to make a sound—transfixed, I guess. But you ask a good question, Nikki—how did they get it in here?" I watched as he continued exploring, poking around the beautiful furniture, that I now noticed—dining room tables and chairs, breakfronts, four-poster beds, chests, and armoires.

"Look here," Mitch called. We joined him standing before a fifteen-foot wide door with rollers that went above it across the ceiling, answering the question of how everything came to be in this space. "I don't dare open it—it might be solid dirt on the other side that could pour right in here on us."

"Right," Alex agreed. "Let's not risk a landslide."

So we turned and worked our way back through the furniture, stopping at the foot of the angel and shining our lights again up at the amazing, white marble face.

"Breath-taking," Yumi whispered.

"Yes," I agreed. Then we quietly turned and made our way back through the mercantile and out to the front porch.

"Wow!" Mitch said softly, shaking his head in disbelief. "I don't think our day of exploring could have been any more productive. Do we want to poke around some more?"

"I think that's about all the input I can handle for one day," I said.

"Agreed," Yumi patted me on the back. "Lots to think about, yes?"

"Yes," I said thinking I had more to think about than she even knew.

Silently, we wended our way back along the boardwalk, up the stairs, into the late afternoon sunlight and made our way to the car.

"Amazing. All of it, so amazing," Alex said softly.

Mitch reached across the front seat and gave me a kiss on my cheek. "You're awful quiet, my pet…."

I snuggled up close to him. "A Yumi said, lots to think about."

"True." He pulled the car back onto the road, and, even though my mind was crowded with thoughts of the library, the mercantile, the amazing, *amazing* angel, and, not least of all, Homer— yet more demanding thoughts of my dad broke through all those clamoring thoughts.

"I … I have to call my dad."

Mitch looked at me, puzzled.

"No, I'm not going to say anything about the underground city."

"How are you going to do that?" Yumi asked.

"Watch me. But, I just … just …."

"Just still feel bad," Mitch finished for me.

"Yes." I dialed Dad's number. "Hey, Bunny-love!" he answered after a couple rings. "What's up?"

"Where are you, Dad?"

"I just landed in Victoria. Walking through the airport on my way to the hotel."

"Oh. Well, Dad, I'm feeling like, kinda lousy not having lunch with you, and all…."

"That's okay, Kitten-boots."

I rolled my eyes as Mitch chuckled. "Kitten-boots! Adding it to my list of endearments…."

"Well, but, Dad, I was thinking, if it works for you, I'd love to meet you for lunch when you come back if you're coming through Seattle."

"*Really?*" I couldn't believe how his voice brightened. "I *am* coming through Seattle, and it for-sure works for me. I have a meeting in the early afternoon tomorrow, and then I'm getting on a plane after that back to O.C. I'd be later in the day, more like dinner-time, if that's okay."

"That's fine, Dad." Then some sort of brainstorm took over my mouth. "In fact, why don't you come home and I'll cook my famous spaghetti dinner for you. You could stay overnight."

An exhalation of surprise issued from all three of my friends.

"Well …" Dad paused. "I could do that. I'd have to leave in the wee hours the next morning in order to get to the office sometime during the day. But I could do that. Okay, here's my Lyft. See you tomorrow, Ladybug. Bye-by."

"Bye, Dad."

"Awww," Mitch teased. "You love your dad, after all, little Ladybug."

Snickering came from the back seat.

"Of course, I love my dad, you big dufus. And, furthermore, that's enough from the peanut gallery."

"I'll be happy to see him," Yumi said. "He's so adorable."

"Often clueless, but adorable," I agreed.

"Will you tell him about the underground city?" Mitch asked.

"Of course not."

"Won't be easy."

"That's why you're all invited to dinner too, to keep the conversation going, without spilling the beans."

"Hmmm, Nikki's famous spaghetti dinner … without spilled beans. Having to keep the lid on a huge confidentiality? Tricky. Which will I choose?" Alex said.

"Spaghetti dinner, of course." I turned my fake-glare on him.

"Probably so. And Mom's cheesecake."

"Even better—thank you!"

Chapter III
The Glowing Angel

Alex invited us to his dad's little deli for a late-lunch-early-dinner, when we got back into town, and we happily agreed. After a lovely meal of Hungarian mushroom soup, imported crackers, fresh, raw, veggies arranged beautifully on a tray, and tea-of-choice, we bid Alex and his dad good-evening, as the three of us piled back into the Chevy, and Mitch drove us the short distance home.

Mitch and I said goodnight at my apartment door—he had to be his attorney internship early in the morning. And I … I needed to get to the mirror and see if there was more information about having seen what looked like Homer there in the morning—which now seemed at least three days ago!

And speaking of Homer, as Mitch and I stood in the hall, Homer came out of Mitch's apartment, looking, it seemed to me, a bit sheepish as he approached us.

"Ah! Young love!" He smiled. "Did you kids have a good day?"

"We had a great day," I answered, and, to forestall any direct questions, I added, "and we just came from Zingas' Grocery where Alex's dad's fed us a lovely supper of Hungarian mushroom soup and veggies and crackers and such. I'm stuffed!"

"Hung mush, my favorite!" Homer grinned. "Well, have a great evening, you two. See you tomorrow."

"Right!" We watched as he continued down the hall to the elevators. That was when I noticed he was wearing street clothes. I'd been trying to figure out what was different about him, but the lack of uniform didn't register right away, given my preoccupation with his guilty expression.

The elevator pinged. As he was about to step in, I called to him. "My dad is coming tomorrow for my famous spaghetti dinner, and staying overnight."

Homer held the elevator door and grinned hugely. "That is great news, I'll be happy to see him!"

"He'll be delighted to see you, too, Homer."

Homer tipped his non-existent hat, and was gone.

I turned to Mitch. "He just came from your apartment."

"He did."

"He was not in uniform."

"Also true."

"Interesting."

Mitch nodded. "And again, true." he kissed me on the tip of my nose, turned, and headed down the hall. "See you tomorrow evening, Kitten-Boots."

"*Arrrg!*" I uttered, turned and I went inside. The apartment was still, and I realized that Yumi had taken herself off to her little bed in the conservatory, and I, for one, was very relieved to—*finally!*—be getting back to my mirror.

*   *

First I changed into my soft, lavender flannel jammies, because of the habit I'd had of late of falling asleep in whatever clothes I had on. Then I went into my closet, closed the door, and sat on the floor in the dark.

Nothing happened. I simply sat in the dark, on the floor, in my pjs, in front of a dark mirror in a dark closet.

Weird, Nikki, I thought to myself. Just go to bed. You know you can't "make" the mirror do anything—other than reflect yourself when there's light.

But, I argued, basically with the mirror, if you want me to do something about Homer, I need more information.

Still, nothing.

"Well, it's early, but I'm tired. I'm going to bed," I said aloud and stood up. Just as I put my hand on the closet door's handle, the sepia roiling began in the mirror, very faintly, in the lower-left corner, and continued to do nothing more than that for a couple of minutes.

Maybe I'm imagining it, I thought. I should just flip on the light, and it'll all go away. But I didn't flip on the light. Instead, I opened the door to go to bed, and as I did so, a blinding light came from the mirror. I shrieked, and put my arm over my eyes.

What. Was. That?

When I opened my eyes, there, in my mirror, stood the amazing, marble angel from the mercantile, in all his glowing glory. I stepped back from the mirror, into my clothes rod. I could not step far enough back to feel comfortable with the angel's intensity.

I didn't know what to say. Or think. Or *do*. Trembling—not, really from fear as much as shock—I sat back down on the floor and watched as the angel sailed to the underground library and right through a window. He came up to the man I thought was Homer, seated at one of the long walnut tables, just like I'd seen him before. The angel shined his great light right on him, while the perspective I was given shifted from the side to in front.

That's when I saw it wasn't Homer. Not exactly. But so much like him as to be readily mistaken for him, dressed impeccably in Victorian clothing. He was clearly distressed. He held his head as he sat at a table filled with open books and a pile of newspapers, a walnut dowel at the fold of each paper. Some of the newspapers were open, some were closed.

The entire ten-foot table was completely covered in newspapers and gigantic books. Apparently, whatever he searched for, he'd not only not found, but it appeared as though it was not to be found.

I wondered how he could not react to the angel, but I guessed he didn't see the glowing presence. Of course! The angel was for my benefit, to draw my attention to the man at the table.

Why? *Why?* What was I to do with this information? What was the point? Why was the Homer-clone so distressed? What was he looking for? And the absolutely most relevant question of all, what could I possibly do for someone nearly one-hundred-and-fifty years in the past?

The tableau in which nothing moved once the Angel had whisked to the library continued with the angel's light on the man, darkness surrounding him.

Look at the books, look at the newspapers, I suddenly told myself. Wouldn't there be clues there?

But even as I had the thought, the image began to fade. The text in the books became faint scribbles. Soon, all was black, and even darker than before, as my eyes had been exposed to the brilliant light of the marble—yet animate!—angel.

He was an angel with an assignment, which my grandmother had taught me when I was a little girl is common among angels. I remembered now that she had told me angels take their assignments quite seriously.

*   *

"Rikki?"

Someone called my name, and I slowly woke up, groggy, disoriented. Where was I? *Oh no!* I was lying on the floor of my closet. That would never do!

Yumi opened the closet door and peeked in.

I scrambled to sit up. Well, at least I was in my pajamas and not the same clothes I'd been wearing the day before.

"What … what are you doing? Are you sleeping on the floor?"

I shrugged sheepishly. "I cannot tell a lie. Yes. I fell asleep on the floor."

She nodded knowingly. "The mirror. It's the mirror. There must have been something in the mirror."

"Well, yes. I cannot tell a lie about that either. But I … I'm not ready to talk about it."

"That's all right. I understand." Yumi nodded, unconvinced. "Ahm, not exactly, no, that's not true. But I won't ask you to tell me anything you don't want to." She turned and left my room. "However, beloved daughter of your doting father, remember he's coming today, and you promised to make him dinner."

Yikes! I completely forgot. "Thanks for the reminder," I called after her thinking that this was one of those many times when I was grateful for her inscrutable-ness. In this case, she didn't try to force me to tell her something I wasn't ready to talk about. And may never be.

I scurried about, making myself ready for the day, with mixed feelings about Dad coming. I discovered that I was really, *really* happy to see him later today, while the major problematic bits were: 1. having to cook a meal for him when my mother was the most amazing cook, and he was a great cook too, and 2. Having him—without the shadow of a doubt!—calling me one of his curious and potentially embarrassing—no, scratch that—*unquestionably embarrassing*—pet names in front of my friends. Which they could use to blackmail me at any time for the rest of my life.

Yes. Torn, I was. But! All I could do was make the best spaghetti dinner that I ever could and ride along on the wave of Dad and friends, however, it may turn out.

Comfortably in sweats, ready the give the apartment a good going over, I went into the hall and dragged out the vacuum—I honestly hadn't seen it since Mom left—and the dusting paraphernalia. Fortunately, we had a fairly decent robot vacuum, but the little guy couldn't get into the corners, and the corners needed to be gotten into.

"Ohh! Let me help, I love to clean!" Yumi took the dust cloth and "lemon fresh" spray cleaner from my hands.

"You're hired, thanks! I also have to give the kitchen a good going over, and check out the plants."

"I told your mother I'd take care of the plants, and I've kept my promise."

"I don't know what I'd do without you." I gave her a virtual hug around the vacuum, then found an outlet for it and turned it on, drowning out further chat.

If anyone had taken a bit of video of us—and, thank goodness, no one did—they would have seen each our own, real, true, character. Yumi methodically, mindfully dusting every inch, taking pride in each movement, and each shining clean surface. Me roaring around the place with the vacuum like I was in a Formula 1 race.

Opposites attract.

Mom would have loved watching Yumi dust each and every key on the piano as if it was a priceless work of art. I had to stop for a moment and appreciate the beauty of the dark wood of the baby grand, complimented by Yumi's gorgeous waist-length hair, almost the same shade of rich, dark brown, as the sun and her dust cloth made silent music across the keys.

I turned off the vacuum, thinking brilliantly. "Ah! Music, that's what we need!" I went to the sound system. "Requests?"

Yumi joined me. "I know!" She brought up a quiet, lovely, but-not-what-I-had-in-mind koto solo.

"Oh. Okay, very nice," I said politely.

"Just. Wait." She softly shook the dust cloth to some un-hearable beat. When, *BOOM!* The unknown-to me-contemporary Japanese band opened like the skies during a thunderstorm. The living room—and probably the whole building!—rocked. We danced around the apartment in utter abandon. No supervision! Nothing to do or think but that the music had us bewitched! *Enchanted!*

Finally, the music wound down and we flopped on the two sofas, grinning and gasping for breath.

"That was *fantastic*, Yumi."

"I'm glad you liked it," she said in her little kitten voice. "It was enjoyable."

"Enjoyable! You are the queen of understatement."

"Is that your phone?"

"Oh!" I got up to retrieve my phone from my room. Mitch had texted me a couple times and Dad had called *three* times.

I called him back. "What's up, Dad?"

"I called you three times!"

"I know. I see that. I didn't listen to the messages, I just called you back. Is something wrong?"

"No. Just giving you progress reports. I'm really looking forward to seeing the apartment, and Yumi and Mitch, and I suppose Alex will be there too. And Homer."

"Wow!" Everyone but me?

I guess he read the tone of my voice.

"Well, you too, of course, before all else, my little snuggle-puppy."

"*Da-a-a-ad!*"

He chuckled, and I realized he'd gotten the rise he was angling for. I couldn't win – if I called him something ridiculous, he'd just – love it. No recourse. "Well, Mr. Creator-of-Snuggle-Puppy, I'm glad you're excited. But stop calling! I'm trying to clean the house and make dinner and whatever else needs doing before you arrive, so let me do it. If you must talk to someone before coming, call Yumi or Homer."

"All righty. Points well made and taken. See you soon! Bye."

I quickly read Mitch's texts, notes of affection, and support. I didn't even have to tell him how this day was affecting me, he got it. I scurried back to Yumi in the living room. "Dad. Calling *three times*. I told him to call you instead. "

"Me!? What would he have to say to me?"

"Probably the same thing he said to me, without the ridiculous name-calling."

"Awww! He's just showing his love."

"Yeah, I know … snuggle-puppy."

Yumi giggled, covering her mouth with her delicate hand, looking up at me with her incredible, luminous eyes. "That's a perfect moniker for you."

"Hmmm. Better yet, I will it to you. It's all yours." I looked around the living room. Aside from our cleaning paraphernalia, it looked great—ready for company. "Okay, let's get the rest of this place pulled together."

We dusted and vacuumed and swept until the apartment looked ready for a photoshoot.

"We're awesome," I proclaimed as we stood in the conservatory by Yumi's little cot. I turned in a full circle to take in the plant-populated room and was surprised to see a couple of the posters I'd gotten for her that I'd put in her room across the hall from mine, here in the conservatory, where she preferred to stay. I didn't know she'd brought the posters in here, pinning them to the only open wall space in the room.

"Oh! Yumi …."

"I had to have my favorite artists with me—of course! I didn't say much when I first saw them, I was so surprised and touched that you'd gotten them. I didn't know you even knew who these artists are. Sometimes, I'm too inscrutable."

"Sometimes." But now, I was inscrutable, as I couldn't find any words for how much it meant to me that she'd put those posters near her. So I turned from them, saying, "All right! Now then, I must organize dinner. It's just spaghetti, but it must be the *best* spaghetti."

I went into the kitchen and took stock of what was already there, making a list of what I needed, then Yumi and I walked to Zingas' grocery, the little bell over the door jangling as we entered.

"Ah! My two favorite young women," Mr. Zingas called to us from the back, stocking shelves.

"Hi, Mr. Zingas," I called, I've got to get a few things for dinner."

"Alex mentioned your dad will be dropping by this evening."

"That's right. And staying overnight."

"And she's stressing about it," Yumi added as we came up to him.

"Well, only because I began to think about what a great cook my mom is, and *what was I thinking cooking for my dad?*"

"I'm certain he's not coming to compare your cooking to your mother's," Mr. Zingas assured.

"No … but …." I trailed off, starting to prowl around the store, getting what I knew I needed, and a bunch of stuff I didn't need.

Yumi continued to chat with Mr. Zingas. For some reason, they really hit it off with each other, which I'd noticed before. Of course, there was now the fact that his son had fallen completely in love with her, and Mr. Zingas was perhaps contemplating the potential of exotically beautiful grandchildren.

"I'm ready," I called from the cash register, where I stood with my two over-full hand baskets.

"Her majesty calls," Mr. Zingas teased as he and Yumi joined me.

"Yes, well, her majesty is ever-closer to a meltdown." I tapped my non-existent watch. "Time flies."

As Mr. Zingas moved around to the front of the cash register, he started to laugh when he saw my pile of goods. "I don't mind making the money, but are you sure you need," he picked up an item, "marzipan paste for your spaghetti dinner?"

"You never know!"

He bagged it all up and, Yumi and I, each taking a bag in hand, bid him good day and headed back to the apartment.

Homer greeted us at the front door. "Goodies for dinner, I'm guessing. Your dad just called me a while ago. He said you told him to call me."

"Only to stop calling me!"

"Well, I'm sorry I might miss him. It sounded like he'll arrive after I'm off for the day."

"Oh. That's too bad. He specifically said he's looking forward to seeing you. Even before saying he looked forward to seeing me."

"His wanting to see you is implicit, Miss Nikki!"

"So he said. But, Homer, if you're around this evening, please stop by."

"I may do that," He smiled and lightly tipped his hat. Yumi and I made our way to the elevators and up to the apartment, plopping the bags down in the kitchen, and ourselves down in the kitchen breakfast nook.

"I'm exhausted, and I haven't even started."

"Me too!" Yumi put her head down on the back of her hands. "You've wiped me out. I'll watch you, now."

"You may. After all, you're my guest. But I bet you won't just sit there."

"No. I bet you're right."

Chapter IV

Nikki's Fabulous Spaghetti Dinner

All too soon, Alex and then Mitch were at the door joining me in the kitchen, the four of us cheerfully under one another's feet.

"My mother sent this packet of spices to put into your spaghetti sauce," Mitch said, handing me a little ziplock bag.

"What's in it?"

"I don't know. Whatever it is, it's bound to be good."

I resisted opening it and taking a sniff. Two thoughts came up: One, I wanted whatever I made—good or bad—to be what I made, and two, what if these spices were just … wrong in my spaghetti?

Mitch frowned at my hesitation. "I'm sure they're not poisonous."

"Of course not. But …."

Alex, astute as always, piped up, "If it *is* poison, Nikki wants it to be her own poison."

"Oh, I get it." Mitch reached to take the spices back, but I wouldn't let him have them. "No … no, I'm going to use them. Your mother was so kind and thoughtful to give me this little packet of her culinary magic, and I'd be both silly and rude not to take advantage of using it."

Mitch smiled. "I'll tell her."

"Yes, please do. Without the hesitation part." I added the mystical packet to my simmering spaghetti sauce, and soon the entire apartment smelled heavenly.

We were all exclaiming about the incredible aroma when I heard Dad call from the front door, "Anybody home?"

I looked at Mitch in horror. "He's early! I haven't even changed!" I rushed to the foyer. It was so good to see him! *"Daddy!"* I cried and threw my arms around him, and he me.

At that moment, I didn't care who saw me or what they thought. This was my own, goofy, wonderful, dad!

"Cuddle Bug," He said hugging me tight. "Wow! Missed you!"

"Me too you," I whispered.

We finally turned, and my three friends were lined up outside the kitchen, watching us with the sweetest expressions on their faces.

Feeling shy, I said, "Enough hug fest! You're so early, Dad!"

"Well, you told me not to call you anymore."

"That'll teach me. I'm disreputable. Haven't showered or changed."

"Doesn't matter sweetie. You're beautiful. Your friends are beautiful." He glanced around the living room, "And the place is beautiful! No graffiti on the walls or anything."

"Well, not in this room, anyway," I teased.

"But—*what* is this amazing aroma?"

"My famous spaghetti dinner, of course! It's just about ready."

"Fantastic. Frankly, I'm starved. I'll just go to my room and freshen up."

"Yumi and I vacuumed and dusted your room. We'll set the table and when you're ready, dinner is served."

"Oh boy!" He said, excited as a little kid as he headed down the hall to his room.

I turned to my friends. "Showtime!"

We dashed about as if we knew what we were doing, setting the table in the lovely dining room. Mitch and Alex brought in a few plants, Yumi lit the candles, and I brought in my masterpiece.

"Spaghetti-a-la-Nikki," I announced as I brought in the sauce, enveloped in its remarkable aroma.

Dad came out of his room, still grinning like a little boy, and soon we were wolfing down my utterly successful meal without a hint of ceremony.

"Just amazing, Nikki," Dad said when we'd all 'licked our platters clean,' and were sitting back, comfortably over-full. "What is this unnamable, extraordinary, flavor?"

"I cannot tell a lie. Mitch's sweet mother sent me a packet of spices, and in they went into the mix. I have no idea what they are. Except, as you say, extraordinary. She's quite the chef." I launched into a recap of the dinner we'd had with her when Homer had joined us too, which Dad had already heard about.

"Yes, she's really changed now that Mitch's terrible uncle is out of the picture," I added.

"How so?"

"Well, she's … she looks a lot like that movie star that Grandpa used to say 'va-va-voom' about."

Dad burst out laughing. "You remember that?"

"I *especially* remember that. I thought Grammy would be jealous. I asked her and she said, no, Grandpa was right. That actress was 'va-va-voom.' I can't remember her name."

"You mean, Sophia Loren?"

"Yeah. That's it."

"You're saying, Mitch's mom looks like Sophia Loren?"

"Pretty much, yeah."

"*Hmmm*," Dad said. I could see his cogs turning. What was he up to?

"I've been meaning to thank her for being willing to help you if you needed anything," he said. "Which clearly you don't! No time like the present. Is she home, Mitch?"

Surprised, Mitch nodded. "Yes, she's home."

"Great!" Dad stood and headed for the front door.

Mitch and I exchanged a look. "I'd better go with him. No telling what he might say, and I need to be witness. I jumped up and headed for the door.

"I'd better go, too," Mitch said, following me.

The three of us made our way the short distance down the hall to the neighboring apartment. As we got to the door, we could hear muted voices. I looked over at Mitch. Who would be with his mom? By his expression, he knew exactly who was in his apartment.

"Homer!" I whispered loudly as dad knocked on the door.

Mitch nodded.

Mitch's mom opened the door.

"Mr. Francis!" She exclaimed, smiling, and yet, obviously a bit uncomfortable. I could see Homer in the background.

"Mrs. Dalca, you're looking great!" Dad gave me the side-long eyeball—*wow!* "I don't want to bother you, but the kids just treated me to the most amazing spaghetti dinner, which I guess some spices of yours went into the mix, I just want to say thank you.

"But more importantly, I want to thank you for simply being here, in case Nikki needed you in any way. Though she's doing a great job of taking care of herself!" He put his arm around me. Then he noticed Homer. "Hey! Homer! My lucky moment, two-for-one, thanks, my friend, for watching out for my little girl!"

Homer took a couple steps toward us, but he, too, appeared a bit uncomfortable. "Nikki's great! She doesn't need any supervision. She's lovely company. Now and then we have a bit of a chat, and she always leaves me smiling!"

"Glad to hear it, glad to hear it." Dad suddenly got a clue. "Well, I won't bother you anymore. You just came up in the conversation because of the delightful spices in the spaghetti, and, as I'm only here a few hours, I wanted to check in and say thanks!"

"I Love Nikki! She's a beautiful person, and is so good for my baby," Mitch's mom said.

"She means me," Mitch observed in a droll tone I'd never heard.

"Indeed I do!"

Ah! I thought with insight. I am not the only person with a parent who could be please-let-me-crawl-under-the-carpet embarrassing.

We made our way quietly back down the hall. But once inside our apartment with the door closed, Dad and I erupted. "*Homer!*" I exclaimed while Dad did a shockingly perfect imitation of my long-passed grandfather, "*Va-va-voom!* is right. Your mom is a knockout, Mitch."

"Yes. Well. She's, you know, *my mom.*"

"Oh, yes. Sorry. Inappropriate. Sorry."

"Augh!" I cried, unable to form actual words. "But, Mitch—*Homer!* Homer is in your apartment again."

"I saw that, yes."

"In off-duty hours."

"Right again, Nikki."

"*Not in uniform!*"

"Your accuracy is astounding."

"What's. Going. On?"

"I think, to some extent, it's none of our business. But they're both Romanian. They both speak Romanian. They've become friends. You started it, Nikki when you insisted that Homer join us for that meal my mother made for us."

"Well, I'm sure it wasn't just that … I mean, Homer has known her for years. Years and years."

"Yes. But that dinner, where they got to be their real selves, informal, sharing warmth, and food from the homeland, and laughter, changed all that."

"*Wow!*" I whispered "*I'm cupid!*"

"Don't go too far—they're just friends."

"But, your mom is amazing, and Homer is amazing, and they're both unattached, and they share strong cultural stuff, and … it's a match made wherever perfect matches are made."

"Mitch is right, Chickie-Luv," Dad added. "They're friends, that's great. Beyond that, we must keep our noses out of it."

"Oh! Right, Dad. You who goes banging on doors without invitation or warning."

"Guilty. Guilty as charged. Whew! What an adventure. I'm ready for dessert!"

We'd formed an animated knot in the foyer, and now turned to see Alex and Yumi in the dining room doorway, bemusement on their faces.

"Sorry to leave you out."

"Oh, we got it," Yumi said. "Surprise! Homer was there, and Mitch's mom is *va-va-voom!*"

*   *

Dad had to leave at five a.m. the next morning, with only about four hours of sleep. After my spaghetti dinner—a one-hundred percent hit, all around!—we'd hunkered down at the living room coffee table, indulging in the multiple crimes of spumoni ice-cream and cheesecake, chatting about everything and nothing. I sat cozily—I have to say it!—like a *cuddle bug*—between my dad and Mitch. *Yum!*

I set my phone alarm for 4:30 a.m. I wanted to walk Dad down to his Lyft, and I surprised him by being at the door when he came out, roller board in hand, ready to sneak away.

"Oh, Bunny Cakes, you didn't have to wake up for me!"

"I know! The fun part is doing it because I want to."

Grinning, he gave me a hug, then we walked down the hall to the elevator and rode down to the street. I was getting kind of used to this business of shuttling parents to the street to be whisked away. But—it still hit a road bump in my emotions. I wanted to be happy because it was a perfect visit. But I was sad. Tears threatened. Because it was a perfect visit.

"Bye, Daddy," I whispered as he climbed into the car that waited at the door.

"Bye, Baby-Mine. You're doing great! I'm so proud. Kisses. Talk soon." And he was gone.

I took a couple deep breaths and turned back to see Homer just taking over his morning shift.

We had to talk! It would be quiet for the next half-hour, and when would there be a more perfect time?

He held the door open for me. "Sad eyes."

"Oh, you know … just always sending parents off lately."

"So it would seem."

"But, Homer … I … we need to talk!"

"What about?"

"Can we step outside?"

"Sure, Miss Nikki." He held the door open and we both stepped outside into the brisk—but not raining—early morning breeze.

"Everything all right?" He asked, looking concerned.

"With me! Yes. But I want to, I need to talk about you!"

"Me? Why?"

"Because I … because you …." Goodness! I should have rehearsed this at least a little bit. I plowed ahead. "I think it's wonderful that you and Mitch's mom have become friends. And, you know, to think that I had a tiny little part in it is very cool, that night when I insisted that you join us for dinner."

"Well, dear Nikki, I suppose you maybe did have a part in it."

But he wasn't smiling like I expected. A shy but happy smile. No. That, I did not see. There was a sadness in his eyes, but, otherwise, his expression was unreadable.

"What, Homer, what's the problem?"

"Oh, you are entirely too perceptive, young miss."

"No, I'm not." Well, maybe I was. But that wasn't the point. The point was, why wasn't Homer happy about the thought of Mitch's mom? And so I asked, "Why aren't you happy about the thought of Mitch's mom?"

"I am …."

"But?"

"I don't know if this is appropriate conversation, Nikki."

I gave him my "steady gaze," daring him to not answer me.

"All right. The short answer is—and Mitch's mom, Relia, doesn't know this—I'm afraid we may be related. Pretty closely related. And, although I have discovered strong feelings for her, and it seems it may be somewhat reciprocal …."

"You *think?*" I interjected a tad sarcastically.

"I'm not willing to change the sweet friendship, which I treasure. Just, Nikki, to be able to chat on occasion in Romanian warms my soul. I don't need it, but it's lovely."

"*Completely* lovely, dear Homer. But, what do you mean, closely related? How can you say that, without knowing for sure?"

"Well," Homer looked inside and down the hall as if expecting to be called to duty that very moment. There was no one to be seen. "Well, her people and my people came over on a ship, perhaps the very same one. My great-great, maybe three greats, uncle Homer came over on a ship as a small child. He became separated from his family when they debarked in New York. He was only five, spoke no English, and he ended up in an orphanage. As soon as he could get away as a young teen, he made his way to the west coast, and ended up here, in Seattle."

"Oh! Sad! How terrible for him and his family."

"Precisely. But, anyway, you see, it's possible, and, in fact, *somewhat likely*, that Relia and I are from the same family."

"*Ohhhhh!*" I said, putting it all together. I paused thinking it through. "But, really, Homer, ahm, I had a bit of genetics in science class last term, and I think that, you know, three generations later, it wouldn't really matter."

"But," Homer said, more emphatically than I'd ever heard this gentle man speak, "*It matters to me. I need to know. I just … I'm stuck, thinking about it, wondering about it. Is it only the fact that we might be related? I don't think so. There seems to be something else that has me hung up.*"

The image of Homer's ancestor, so real, so troubled, appearing in my mirror came to me. "Maybe your ancestor is still—troubled. Maybe he needs you to resolve this question *for him*."

Homer raised his eyebrows. "Are you saying you believe in ghosts?"

"I believe in energy. I believe that when a person evacuates a body, they continue on. They don't die.

But they may have a need for some closure here, in the three dimensions."

"Evacuates a body!" He chuckled, giving me a quizzical look. "Now, *that's* interesting!"

Right then a couple stepped through the door, and Homer snapped to attention. Where did they come from? "Gotta mind my station, Nikki," he said, attending to the door.

"I'm going to do some research on your problem, Homer."

"Oh, don't trouble yourself, Miss Nikki."

"Not trouble! No, it'll be fun and exciting."

I hurried back up to the apartment. Would the mirror provide me more clues?

Chapter V
Glowing Numbers

Relieved that all was still when I stepped into the apartment, I went straight to my room, into the closet, and closed the door. Although I knew it was unlikely that the mirror would do anything other than show me a faint reflection of myself in the thin light from under the door, I was prepared to wait patiently. I now had an idea what Homer's ancestor uncle was distressed about and what he was looking for, I could focus on meaningful details.

But I didn't have to wait after all. It was as if the mirror had been waiting impatiently for me. I saw a soft glow of light, dead center in the mirror. At first I thought it was probably just the light from under the door catching on something and making a reflection. But no. The light grew in intensity, and soon it appeared as if I was in the Victorian underground library.

As much as I knew I needed to stay focused on the task at hand, I still could not resist becoming fascinated with the rich, dark woods, and the light streaming in from the tall windows. A sunny day in Seattle! They apparently had them then, too, on occasion!

But the glow grew to a bright light, and the faint outline of the stunning stone angel began to appear at a distance. As it moved, the entire picture moved with it. Soon I faced a row of neatly bound books, on their spines a sequential range of numbers. The angel, now behind me, cast a laser beam of light upon one particular spine, where the gold lettering against its dark burgundy cover fairly sparkled: 1249-2400.

And then, *Slam!* The entire image shut off as if a switch had been flipped.

I sat in the darkness, contemplating the angel, the library, and the glowing numbers I would never forget.

*   *

I couldn't wait for everyone to wake up and to get the day in motion. Mitch was off from his internship today, and we could perhaps talk Mr. Zingas into letting Alex off early.

I went into the kitchen to make myself some hot oatmeal. I don't know why except I had the idea that I ought to be well-fortified for the day ahead. I made an undue amount of noise banging the pans and dishes and silverware about more than necessary, in the hopes that it got Yumi up. It worked.

"Why are you making all this racket?" She stumbled into the kitchen in her *Hello Kitty* pajamas, hair awry, and a pillow crease across her cheek. *How? I* had to stop and wonder, how does she manage to look so darn adorable, half-asleep? When I first wake up, I look like I've been in a boxing match with Bozo the clown and lost.

"Oh! Sorry, Yumi. I got inspired to make hot oatmeal, and have been digging out everything I need."

"Hot oatmeal? You hate oatmeal." She sat at the little kitchen breakfast nook bench seat facing my whirlwind activity.

"True. But maybe I don't still hate it. I haven't had it in years, and since both of my parents like it, maybe it's something you grow into. Anyway, I need to be fortified for the day. Want some oatmeal?"

"Yeah. Sure. If you have brown sugar."

"I do! I'm pretty sure I'd still turn up my nose at oatmeal without it."

"Oatmeal is good for you," Yumi said, as if I'd never heard that very line one-thousand-times-one-thousand from my parents.

"Yumi states the obvious," I teased.

"Hey, the sun is barely up, and I'm still asleep."

I wanted to chuckle, but in fact, I felt guilty.

"I apologize for waking you. I kinda meant to, but now I feel bad. Go back to bed!"

Yumi laughed her sweet little laugh. "You're so silly! I'm up now, and, surprising wonder-of-wonders *you're cooking oatmeal.* I need to know what's going on in that ever-churning mind of yours."

"Ever-churning. Hmmm, making butter, I guess." I had to attend to what I was doing for a minute as the water boiled, and I stirred the oatmeal into it. "Lookin' good!" I'd never made oatmeal before—and always resisted eating it. But I proved I was capable of reading directions.

"Oh, wait!" Yumi exclaimed. "Goodness, I really am tired! That's why you're up so early, to see your dad off."

"Yes. And I did. He said he was proud of me."

"Well, of course, Nikki. Of course he's proud of you."

"But it was nice to hear."

"Sure." Yumi got up and gathered the dishes and silverware and set the table. Soon we were settled in with our hearty breakfast. "So, Nikki, what's the plan for the day? It must be spectacular."

"Oh. Well. Spectacular, that's a bit strong." I thought about the expression on Homer's face just a short while ago as he mentioned his feelings for Mitch's mom, and I knew that my hopes for the day were, in truth, nothing less than spectacular. "Nope. on second thought, spectacular is just about right."

"I'm listening."

I piled more than necessary—but what's necessary?—brown sugar on my oatmeal, stirred in some oat milk, my new favorite, and took a cautious spoonful. "Wow! Hey, that's not half bad."

"No," Yumi agreed, having already nearly finished a bowlful. "Quite tasty. I may have some more."

"Please do," I answered, shocked. Yumi never had seconds of *anything*. Except, of course, Alex's mom's cheesecake. *And now, my oatmeal!* I had reached an important plateau of some sort. Not sure, what exactly, but there it was. I got up and served her more oatmeal, glad I'd cooked up a good-sized batch.

Yumi sat grinning as I topped up her bowl.

"What's so funny?"

"You serving me! It's funny and lovely," she said softly.

"You're funny and lovely," I retorted, turning off the stove and setting the nearly empty pan of oatmeal back on it.

"Thank you! Now then, please let me in on the spectacular events that are to unfold today."

I hesitated. Of course I wanted to tell Yumi everything, the whole, romantic story, and my hopes of being helpful. But what if I wasn't able to be helpful? And, even more importantly, was Homer's story mine to tell to anyone, even Yumi? No. Not at this moment.

Though the little grey cat had been instrumental in discovering Yumi's historical tie to the underground city, I couldn't be sure that the angel was going to result in the same sort of outcome for Homer.

"I can't tell you, just yet, Yumi."

"Ohhhh! The mirror."

"Yes. The mirror. And I need to follow up on something in the underground city."

"A big day exploring?"

"A big day exploring."

Yumi got up and washed her dishes. "I'm getting dressed and calling Alex. I hope his dad will let him off work early. We don't want to go without him, do we?"

"We do not," I agreed, contemplating the locked gate on the boardwalk to the library. We'd need all of our brain and body power!

*   *

𝕴 gathered Dad's tools, then called Mitch to give him a sketch of my plans for the day and to remind him about the library gate so he could bring any tools he might have that could be useful opening it. "Do you think we'll need to buy any tools before we get there?"

"I don't know, Nikki. Let's just take it slow and be patient. If we don't get through the gate today, we can do it some other time."

That was not the answer I was prepared to accept, but I decided to at least try to sound like I agreed with him. "Hopefully we have all the tools we'll need, I guess." Yumi came into my room, dressed, with her backpack on. "We're ready any time you are, Mitch."

"What about Alex?"

"What about Alex?" I asked.

"He's walking over to Mitch's car right now," Yumi said.

"I heard that," Mitch said. "All right, so much for my beauty sleep. I'll be ready in a few."

I hung up then opened my backpack, pulling out my flashlight and my new headlamp I'd gotten, flipping them on to make sure they both worked. "Let's go down to the car." I pulled on my backpack and picked up the tool bag.

"All right," Yumi agreed. "But, hmmm, I've never seen you miss a chance to be by Mitch's side!"

"I know, but I'm just … antsy. I don't want him to see my, ahm, energy until we're on the road, or he'll go on about *patience*."

Yumi giggled. "Oh. Patience. Not an entirely bad idea."

"Don't you start!" We stepped outside the apartment and I closed the front door, checking to make sure it was locked. We walked down the hall to the elevators.

Just as the elevator pinged and the doors slid open, Mitch came out of his apartment, backpack on his back and tool bag in hand. I held the door while he joined us.

"You weren't going to wait for me?"

"Yes. At the car." I kissed him on the cheek.

"You weren't even going to wait for me. My comment about patience was unheard."

"Wrong. It was heard. Just not heeded," I corrected, laughing.

"She's antsy," Yumi offered.

"I see. Any reason for a particularly heightened antsy?"

"Yes, Sweetie. But, for the moment, I must remain discrete."

"Oh. Something in the mirror."

"Yes. Something in the mirror."

As we stepped off the elevator, Homer, attending to Mrs. Wishkener at the door, gave us a small nod and a smile. The three of us waved back. Outside in the beautiful, sunny day just made me feel like everything would fall neatly into place. I had a mission, I was with my best-best friends, and my dad was proud of me.

Perfect! Okay. That all made me a bit uncomfortable. *Toooo* much opportunity for things to not be perfect.

We joined Alex, who leaned against Mitch's Chevy. "Finally! I thought I was going to have to go up and drag you from your nests." He pulled Yumi to him, burying his face in her hair. "Missed my girl," I heard him whisper.

Oh, my heart filled with joy to see this sweetness.

"Well, I almost missed my girl, too," Mitch said. "Running off without me."

"What?" Alex frowned.

"He needs to go on because Nikki was at the elevator and intended to come down to the car without him, when he happened to step into the hall as the elevator doors opened," Yumi said.

"Whoa!" Alex observed. "Nikki's on a mission."

"Nikki is," I agreed, as we stowed our backpacks and tools in the cavernous trunk. "Let's hit the road!"

"Let's!" Yumi chimed in. "Such a beautiful day! Summertime and sunshine in Seattle, and an underground city to explore." She paused. "That doesn't make much sense. Why are we going underground on this beautiful day?"

"There'll be sunshine when we come back out," I said, hoping I wasn't telling a fib.

"It could be raining," Yumi caught me out.

"And we'll love the rain, too."

"Somewhat strangely, I have come to love the rain."

"Rain is lovely for cuddling." I scooched closer to Mitch to prove my point.

"Right, *Cuddle Bug*," he said trying to ruffle my feathers with Dad's endearment.

But no feathers on this bug! We were on the road, my mission was clear—well, pretty clear—and the most gorgeous young man in the world was teasing me. "I'm *your* Cuddle Bug. Hmmm—I guess, technically, I'm my dad's cuddle bug first. But I'm yours, second."

"I'm good with that." Mitch grinned like the family picture I made with him in it made him particularly happy.

We fell into a silent reverie for the rest of the drive, drinking in the day. For my part, I puzzled over how to get through the beautiful locked arch that kept me from going into the library....

Chapter VI

The Fork in the Road

As the familiar surrounding scenery and then the grassy hillside came into view, I became both calmer and, at the same time, more excited. But the antsy feeling faded away. I was here, now, I had my mission, I had my friends, we were good to go.

Mitch pulled onto the hillside and we all clambered out, stretching and gathering our paraphernalia from the trunk. We had done this enough times now that Mitch and I didn't need to advise Alex and Yumi to be cautious. We went down the dirt steps, stopping, as always, to give Millie a reverent moment, and then continued on.

I never, *ever* tired of seeing the first few houses, reminding me of how I fell in love with Mitch, and he with me, especially this porch that we just now passed, where we went through so much anxiety and pain, and where we learned so much about each other. That wonderful moment when neither one of us could deny the feelings that had grown between us—curious as they may be, the feelings of love.

Mitch and I stopped for a moment and exchanged a glance in the near-darkness, sharing unspoken words. And then the four of us continued on the boardwalk.

Finally, we came to Yumi's ancestor's house—goodness, it seemed like it took a long time to get here! I guess I was still a bit more anxious to be at the library than I thought.

We walked and walked, our flashlights trained on the boardwalk, saying little other than to mention a weak spot, or some other small, incidental detail.

Then, so much farther than it had seemed before, I saw the mercantile come into view, up its small incline. "My goodness, that took a long time!" I exclaimed. "It seems as if it was at least twice as far as before."

"It's always like that," Mitch observed. "When you don't know something is coming, it's a surprise, and it seems like it happened right away. But when you're watching for something that you know is there, it seems to take longer."

"I'll try to remember that. But then, how many eons and miles away is the library?"

"I think it's just ahead, only two eons," Alex said. "Are we going to poke around in the mercantile?"

"I believe Nikki is inflexibly focused on getting into the library," Mitch said.

"That's correct." I moved ahead of the group. "Onward. The mercantile is not going anywhere."

"Neither is the library," Alex noted, but he followed along.

We needed now to concentrate more fully on the boardwalk as, not only was it less familiar, but it was less stable, and the surroundings were ever more dark. I remembered this part, the pervasive darkness.

"The fork in the road," Mitch said softly when we came to it.

"Yes. The fork in the road."

We stood at the fork for a few moments, all our lights trained on the left path. I reached up and turned on my headlight, which I'd not felt we needed until now.

Mitch shone his light on further down the boardwalk, and there, faintly, we saw the outline of the beautiful Victorian black wrought iron seven-foot arch and its locked gate. As we stood there, lost in thought, Mitch began to chuckle, and then to laugh outright.

I looked at him in stupefied mystification

"Well, what's so dang funny?" Alex asked.

"Nikki was so concerned about whether we had the tools we needed to break the lock, and we both brought every tool we have … neither one of us remembering," he flashed his light back along the boardwalk, "the mercantile—chock full of tools."

"*Ohhhh!*" I sighed. "I can't believe me. How did that slip my mind? Funny! All right then, we're good to go! So … let's go!" I pushed past my three friends.

"Carefully, Nikki!" Mitch called. "We won't accomplish anything if you fall off or through the boardwalk, and I have to rush you to have a broken bone set. You won't be down here for *months* if that happens."

I stopped in my tracks. He was wise and right as always.

They came up to me and we continued to the archway.

"So beautiful, so delicate," Yumi said. "I really do hope you don't have to damage its beauty."

"We won't," I said, hoping against hope that didn't turn out to be a lie.

Mitch handed me his flashlight. I trained both his light and mine, as well as my headlight, on what appeared to be the lock mechanism. "Well," he said, "here's what looks to be a keyhole, but even it is pretty ornate, it has filigree over the keyhole. I have no idea how a key could fit in it."

"Really?" I got as close to the mechanism as Mitch was, and head-to-head, we studied the intricate mystery. There was, for sure, decorative filigree over what looked like a keyhole, which I couldn't see until I was as close to it as Mitch. "It's some kind of puzzle. Why is it here? I mean, is a library the sort of place where people want to break and enter and steal? You can check stuff out during regular hours."

"I think it's probably more of an esthetic statement," Mitch said. "We can't see it now, but I've been thinking about this gate, and I believe there was likely a botanical garden on the other side of the gate."

I waved my flashlight into the darkness. No doubt Mitch was right. I saw no buildings, but only a small hill, slightly more black in the overwhelming blackness that surrounded us.

"I think you're right. So—maybe this gate isn't really locked as much as having some sort of clever combination or … something … to open it." I touched the filigree on the keyhole and felt a slight give. I followed some weird inner direction or intuition and pushed the filigree to the left, then to the right, and, again, felt something give under my touch. I moved my finger to the left again, and with a surprising, gently whine, the gate swung open.

"O.M.G., Nikki," Yumi exclaimed. "Just, *magic!*"

"No. I felt something give and I just followed that feeling."

"Yeah," Alex said, "Like Yumi says, 'magic.'"

"Pretty impressive," Mitch agreed.

I didn't know what to say, so I said nothing. It seemed, almost, that they were right. I stepped through the gate, and everyone trained their light on the path before me. I took three, then four steps and turned to look up the small hill at the library.

"Ohhh!" I gasped—the angel stood in the library's doorway, glowing.

"What, Nikki?" Mitch asked anxiously.

"The angel! Don't you see the angel?"

No one said a word, then finally Mitch said, "No, Nikki, I don't see the angel. You don't see it, do you?"

Both Yumi and Alex mumbled to the negative.

I looked back up at the library, and the angel was gone. Well, I saw it and it was there. My three friends were focused on watching me, walking in the dark, on the boardwalk. I turned my light onto the hillside, looking for the path. I soon found it and followed my light down to where it joined the boardwalk. It was a beautiful stone pathway, even in the darkness, the path was so sweet-looking, so … so Victorian, like out of a watercolor of long ago.

"Come along," I urged my companions, not waiting to see if they did or not. I walked up the gentle incline to two steps, another stretch of gentle incline, and another two steps. Yet a third gentle incline, and I was at the three steps of the wide front porch, with a wide double door in the center. Stepping up on the porch, I training my headlight and my flashlight on the wooden floor, checking to see if it had any obvious gaping holes, then I stepped up on it cautiously, and crept to the door.

I heard my friends following, exclaiming about the pretty path, and admonishing one another to step carefully.

In the dark it looked like there were four rocking chairs on the porch, dark wood with rattan seats and backs. At least those were the details of the one closest to me. I had an urge to sit in it, but not only was I not sure if it was still sturdy and would sustain my weight, I had to stay focused. I wondered at the strangely, strong urge to plop myself down in that rocking chair, at that very moment.

Mitch, Yumi, and Alex joined me.

"Look at the lovely rocking chair," Yumi said. "I feel like sitting down in it, right here, right now."

"Interesting. I had the same urge. But let's press on. We'll relax in the rocking chairs in the mid-afternoon sun with our mint juleps after our chores are done."

"Minus the sun," Alex observed.

"Well, yes. If you want to be a stickler for details, minus the sun. Minus the mint juleps, too, probably."

Mitch rattled the door handle. "Locked. No surprise. You want to touch it, Nikki, and see if it'll fly open?"

"Very funny."

"Half-joking, half-serious. I think our tools might now come in handy." He set his tool bag on the floor and opened it, then thrashed around, pulling out a screwdriver.

"What do you have in mind?" I asked.

"I'm hoping," he said, putting the screwdriver between the two sections of the door at the lock, "that I'll be able to wiggle the lock mechanism loose. It might not take too much." He struggled with it for a few minutes while Alex, Yumi, and I stood in breathless anticipation.

"It's not giving," I observed, stating the obvious.

"True," Mitch agreed. He paused.

I thrashed around in his tool bag and pulled out a can of PB Blaster. "This might be helpful. Let's spray the lock and wait a few minutes for it to work."

"Good idea." Mitch stepped back and I sprayed the keyhole and the slit in the door. Then Yumi and I cautiously sat in a couple of the rocking chairs, which held our weight, while Mitch and Alex sat on the floor in front of us. Except for the pitch darkness, it was all very cozy.

But after a couple minutes, I got up, grabbed the screwdriver, and imitated the way Mitch had been working at the door. I saw a glow on the other side of the beveled glass windows in the mahogany door, and I knew the angel waited for me.

"I think it's a bit soon," Mitch suggested. At the same moment, I heard a slight, "*click!*"

I turned the handle, and the door opened.

"Why do I even speak?" Mitch shrugged.

We all passed through the tall double doors into the library-smells-of-all-library-smells.

"Ummm," Alex whispered, "*Books! Old books!*"

"Yes, very old books." Our lights played over the walls of books. Magnificent! In a time of no cars and no planes, thousand and thousands of books had managed to find their way into this Seattle Library.

As much as I would have loved to poke around and discover books I'd like to read for myself, right now I had to find a row of large, burgundy-covered books with sequential ranges of numbers on each.

My friends had scattered, each intrigued by a different section. "If anyone happens to find a row of large books with burgundy covers and gold numbers on their spines, let me know. That's what I'm looking for."

"Will do," Mitch said, while Yumi and Alex were so caught up in their exploration, they didn't even respond. I wasn't sure they heard me.

I looked around the room for the angel. I finally saw a glow in an alcove at the opposite end of the library. Making my way down the aisle between the long walnut tables and walnut chairs—the very ones I'd seen in the vision—I finally came to the alcove, and as I approached, the glow became stronger.

Then the angel appeared, much smaller, it had shrunken to fit in this little alcove. I turned my light on the rows of books, and there, somewhat predictably, was what I looked for—a row of large burgundy books with gold numbers on their spines.

I ran my light along the spines, looking for 1249-2400. Even though I saw those numbers glowing on one of the books, I obstinately looked at each spine until I came to it. I couldn't help remembering the purple hat that fell to dust the moment Yumi touched it in *Millie's Millinery*, and I feared the same would happen now, with this precious book. If it crumbled at my touch, what would I do?

I had to believe that this book held significant information the angel wanted me to know, about Homer's Great, Great, Great Uncle's dilemma, and perhaps Homer's dilemma, as well. I reached out and very, *very* gently touched the spine of the book furthest from the one I needed to open. It didn't crumble! It felt quite solid. I'd actually had the foresight to pack a pair of cotton gloves. I took my backpack off and rummaged through it for them, then pulled them on.

Slowly, inch by inch, I pulled the book from the shelf, and with a soft swoosh, I had it in my hands. Good enough! Now for the book I actually needed. I concentrated with every nerve-end as I slid the book from the shelf even more slowly than the other. Finally, there it was, in my hands.

"What have you found?" Mitch asked.

Startled out of my skin, I nearly threw the book from my hands. "Holy Frankenstein, Mitch, give a girl some warning."

"I've been calling your name for five minutes. I didn't see you back here in this dark corner."

"Dark corner?" Oh, that's right, my friends could not see the angel's light. "I saw the angel in this alcove, and here's what I'm looking for." I held the book like I was holding a butterfly in my hands.

"Why are you holding it like that?"

"The purple hat."

"Oh! Right."

"I first got out that book," I pointed with my nose. "And it stayed intact. I was concentrating on this one, the one I need, when you snuck up on me and scared me witless."

"Not snuck, Nikki. Things are potentially scary enough down here in the dark, without *trying* to scare you."

"You succeeded without trying, then. Anyway, let me move to a table where I can see if I can figure out why this book is important to the cause."

"What cause?"

"The cause you will eventually know all about, but which, at present, is a confidence that belongs to someone else. It's not mine to tell—yet."

"Fair enough." Mitch stepped aside, and I went through the little arched doorway of the alcove and put the book on the table with a sigh of relief. That much accomplished!

I turned around in a full circle, looking for the angel, but his light had completely disappeared. Pulling out a chair that had not been sat in for over one-hundred-and-forty years, I sat and opened to the flyleaf, where I saw written in big, ornate letters:

Real Estate Ownership Records – 1249-2400.

What would I find here? The volume was massive, and, turning to an interior page, the print was very small.

"What are you looking for?" Mitch asked.

"I was just asking myself that question. I don't know. I was all excited, but now …."

"Maybe there's some sort of index in the back."

"Good idea." I closed the book and turned it over, then opened to the last few pages. "Oh! Mitch, you're brilliant!" I knew now what I was looking for, as I saw a list of names. "Such tiny print! Hold the light close."

Mitch brought his flashlight close to the page and I adjusted my headlamp. I turned to the "M's," then "Muller," and there it was—Homer Muller. "Yes!"

Mitch leaned in close. "Homer Muller? That's Homer's name."

"Indeed, it is. And now we'll see what land he owned."

"Oh, my goodness, Nikki. Are you going to find a treasure for Homer like you did Yumi's mom?"

"Not exactly. I'm looking for a different sort of treasure. Something that will make him very happy, if I can find it. But first things first. What property did his ancestor uncle own, and will we be able to get to it?" I squinted at the page to see what page was referenced, and then carefully, patiently-impatient, turned to the page, because, although the book had not fallen apart, the pages felt brittle, even through my gloves.

Yumi and Alex joined us. "What did you find?" Yumi asked.

"She's incredible," Mitch said. "I don't know how she does it …."

"The angel," I interjected.

"Okay, the angel led her to this giant book, and she's now looking for the property that Homer's Great, Great, however many Greats Uncle owned."

"Hoping to go there?" Alex asked.

"Right."

"Good luck with that!"

"*Yikes! Great luck! Listen to this!*" I began to read, "'Property at blah-blah-blah-big-long-legal-description, in the present ownership of Homer Muller, to be developed into *Seattle Mercantile*. The store structure, plans at more-blah-blah, include a first-level store front, blah-blah a bunch of measurements, with storage space of a bunch more measurements, and a roll-up door for entrance and egress of furniture and other larger items.'" I read quietly for a moment. "Oh, we missed this altogether when we were there. 'Structure to include second level living quarters, inclusive of bedroom, living room, kitchen, and bath.' And dimensions of each of the rooms.

"I wonder how you get to the second story?"

"I noticed a little window on the second level," Yumi said, "but I thought it was the attic."

"I didn't notice it," I mused, disappointed in myself. I liked to think details like that didn't get by me. And, apparently, another even more significant detail got by us all—a stairway to the second floor!

"Let's go!" Alex urged. "This is so fantastic."

"You just want to go back to the mercantile," I chided.

"True, my genius sleuth-ing friend. But, even more, I want to find the invisible stairway. None of us saw it, right?"

"I didn't see a stairway, not at all. Like I say, I saw that little window and had the thought that the building had an attic, with probably a hole in the ceiling somewhere, which, of course, we weren't looking for," Yumi said.

Mitch shook his head. "I didn't see a stairway, and, as I was poking around the building while you three hooligans were gawking at the goods, I'm surprised I didn't. The place is not so big that a stairway could get by every one of us."

"Gorgeous, intriguing, *Victorian* goods," I emphasized.

"Yes. Gorgeous, intriguing Victorian goods," Yumi repeated, thinking, I knew for sure, of the delicate, "gorgeous and intriguing" chatelaine.

"I stand appropriately corrected," Mitch feigned diffidence.

"Enough chit-chat. Let's go find a stairway—and whatever else we're looking for," Alex urged.

"Wait a minute, just wait a minute. Let me think." Something needed to be done. What was it? Yes, I had to put the two books back, neat and safe and sound. But there was something else. "Oh, yes, of course. I need to keep this information. It might be important aboveground."

"Right, right, right, " the three of them agreed.

They all pulled out chairs around me and sat while I got out my phone and recorded the entire, detailed description into it, and then I emailed the audio file to myself to make doubly sure I had it.

Then I stood and, taking my time, I carefully replaced both big burgundy books on their timeless shelf. "Now we're ready to go!"

Chapter VII
Looking for a Stairway

Mitch gathered his tools, and we closed the door to the library, leaving it unlocked, fairly certain no vandals were likely to come along. We had a bit of a debate about closing the archway gate on the boardwalk—I feared if we closed it, it would lock, and I might not have the same "magic" next time, feeling the locking mechanism under my finger.

Finally, Mitch came up with the clever, if somewhat obvious, idea of getting a rock from the pathway to the library and putting it in the way of the arch gate so it could not close all the way, and then we were on our way to the mercantile. Correction, Homer's ancestor's mercantile.

So strange! It seemed like the mercantile was practically right next door, now, on the return. "I wonder if it's being in the dark …." I mused when the mercantile soon came into view.

"If what's being in the dark?"

"The weirdness with distance. I complained about how far it was when we came down, and now it seems ridiculously close upon returning."

"On the way, you didn't know what you were looking for," Mitch said, "So you were more anxious than you are now when you have what you're looking for."

"Still anxious," I answered. "Even though I got this very significant hunk of information, I don't have any information about the real issue. Okay, I must shut up now, or I'm going to be talking about something that, at this moment, is not mine to discuss."

"Well, it's about Homer, that much has been revealed," Yumi noted. But, beyond that, we'll just stay focused on the boardwalk. We needn't think about other details right now."

"Well said, Yumi." I hoped that once in the upstairs apartment—even if we had to take one of the ladders from the store and lean it up to the little attic window that Yumi had noticed and I hadn't, to get there—once there, I'd find something that would really, truly be of benefit to Homer.

Single file, led by Mitch, we walked into the mercantile and looked around in the store section of the building. There was no stairway here, nor even a place for one if he'd wanted it in here.

Casting our lights all about us, we walked through the narrow hall. Of course, there was no stairway here, in the hall. Then we came into the storage room, with its beautiful furniture and the stunning angel.

I moved to stand under him. "Are you not going to show us the stairway? You led me to all of this information I have, and then you'll just leave me hanging?"

The angel looked down at me with his incredible face, so beautiful, but so dispassionate. Although looking right at me, his expression seemed to be one of an entity who could not be bothered with my little human concerns.

Maybe that was true, but then, why lead me all over the place, giving me so much information? I was missing something.

"Here's my intuition," Mitch said, coming up to me and putting his arm around me, "I think you're supposed to discover the rest of the mystery on your own. It wouldn't mean as much to you if it was all handed to you, would it?"

"I don't know. I'll have to ponder that. But right now, I want to help someone I care about, and I'll take any and all the assistance. I'm not a bit proud about that."

Mitch chuckled. "I still think I'm right. We can find the stairway on our own."

"And we *will* find the stairway on our own," Alex added.

But no! We scoured the place, and there was, simply, *no stairway*.

"He must have changed his plans from what was written in the burgundy book," I said, discouraged as we finally all plopped down in dining room chairs at a round oak dining room table.

"Yes. He must," Yumi agreed. "Maybe we can find that in the big burgundy books," she said hopefully.

"That's a thought," I said, not happy. I put my head down on my crossed arms, turning my head to the right, facing the dark back wall, and the gigantic rolling door. Back in the corner of the building, I saw an outline on the wall.

"What?...." I got up and wandered into the farthest corner of the building. Sure enough, when I got right up to it, there was a plain door, no window, hardly any molding, nearly invisible. I tried the tiny latch on the door, and it opened. I stepped "outside" and flashed my light around to my right, and then to my left.

And there, built against the outside of the building, I found a flight of stairs to the second floor.

Grinning I stepped back inside, "Come along you bunch of lazies. I need some assistance."

*   *

Everyone came tumbling through the door, exclaiming as they stood gaping up at the stairs that went over our heads.

"How did I miss this door before?" Mitch asked in amazement.

"I saw it," Yumi said, "but I thought it looked like a closet door. And we weren't looking for a stairway, then," Yumi said.

Alex shook his head like he felt too stupid to believe himself.

"I don't know how we all missed it, but we've got it now. Let's go!" I ran around to the bottom step.

"Carefully, Nikki," Mitch said. "We don't have any idea about the strength of these ancient stairs."

"I wasn't even thinking, I'm so excited, but you're right, Mitch. These stairs were initially outside in the elements, and have been in this damp environment for a long …."

"Very long!"Alex interjected….

"Very, very, long time," I agreed.

"I should try them,"Yumi said. "I'm the smallest person, and also the most dispensable."

"Whoa!" I protested. "No, and no!"

Mitch and Alex added their sounds of protest.

"But it's true. If I fell through, I'm the easiest one to carry back."

I stepped away from the stairs. "Okay. This is getting … no, that's too much. An adventure, all right. A strong possibility of harm to any of us? No. That's not all right. I'm not doing it, and I'm not letting any of you do it."

As I babbled on, Mitch went inside the mercantile, and soon came out with a tall ladder. Alex scurried to help him heft it against the wall.

"Fortunately, there's a hardware store nearby," Mitch said.

"Fortunately," I agreed, both chagrined and delighted.

"I'd rather go up the stairs," Yumi said quietly.

I looked at her and saw her giving the ladder a look of apprehension.

Then I looked at the ladder, and thought about climbing it, and had a similar feeling. Stairs: good. Ladder: scary.

"I'm on ladders all the time," Alex said. "I have no problem with it. This isn't even very high. I'll go up and … hmmm, what, Nikki? What do you have in mind that we're doing, once up there?"

"Well, I'm looking for something—for details about Homer-the-First's life. I don't know, I'll know it when I see it."

"But if I'm the only one who goes up there, you won't know it when I see it."

"Plus," Mitch added, "The door may be locked."

"The door may be locked," I repeated. "We have tools, so that's probably not as big a problem as climbing the ladder. How do you feel about climbing the ladder, Mitch?"

"Well, I'm not as casual about it as Alex, but I'll do it. Or I could try the stairs. The railing is metal pipe, so even if the stair gave away, I'd be able to hang on and get on another step."

"We have a plan," I announced. "Alex will climb the ladder, test the stair landing, see if it'll hold weight while he still has the security of the ladder, and see if the door's locked. He's right, it's really not very far up. Really."

"Yeah. Not until you're up there looking down," Alex laughed. "But I've done it lots, painting our house. Okay, I'm going up." He fussed around with situating the ladder some more until it was absolutely steady, and slowly, up he went.

He had to crawl under the railing around the landing. Then he held onto the metal railing and stomped on the landing. "Wow! Really solid," he called down.

He tried the door. "Yep, door's locked." He leaned down and looked at the lock. "It looks like a simple skeleton key lock. There's a hoop of skeleton keys in the store, Mitch. Did you see them?"

"Ahm, no. Where are they?"

"By the cash register."

"I'll be right back."

While Mitch was inside, Alex tried the top step. "Also feels solid!"

"Don't," Yumi called. "You're scaring me!"

"Don't be scared my little pet. I'm holding onto the railing, and … whoops!" The next step down made a cracking sound. "Hmmm. Guess I'll wait on the landing. I think it's probably okay, but there's no need to push it if Nikki is willing to come up the ladder. You'll just have to hang out there, Yumi."

"Maybe the steps are safe for me."

Mitch rejoined us, jangling a giant round ring of long, skinny keys. "I'm going up." He put the ring over his forearm and started to climb. When he got close enough for Alex to reach the keys, he handed them to him, then went up a couple more steps on the ladder before stopping and turning on his flashlight, shining it on the lock, as Alex started to try the keys.

"The keys all look the same, but I guess there must be some subtle difference as they feel a bit different. Nothing's working … oh, yay! Here we go!" The door opened and Alex disappeared into an apartment that no one had entered in many decades.

"Now me," Mitch said, ducking under the railing, and crossing the threshold.

"And now me," I said, glancing at Yumi. "Wish me luck."

"Don't do it if you don't feel safe, Nikki."

"Well, dear Yumi, I wouldn't be here at all if I was not to do something that didn't feel safe! Give me some light." Yumi shined her flashlight on the bottom steps of the ladder, and I watched my feet very carefully, as I took one step and then the next. I didn't look at the ground, and I didn't look up. I just looked at my feet. I was shocked when in a few moments, I was eye level with the landing.

"Good work Nikki!" Yumi exclaimed.

"I'm not in yet." I carefully crossed under the railing and stood. "Don't go anywhere!" I called down, teasing.

"Okay! I won't."

I stepped into the dark little apartment just as Alex lit a kerosene lantern. "Let there be light!" he intoned.

"Good job," Mitch said.

I came up behind Mitch. "Is it safe?" I asked.

"*Yikes!*" Mitch yelled. "Sheesh, Nikki, give a guy a warning!"

"*Touche´!*" I crowed. I hadn't intended to startle him, but it was good karma for the library scare he'd given me.

"You made it!" Alex put the kerosene lantern on a little table, where it lit the entire small room.

"I did. And I'm wondering if the lantern is safe to burn in the underground."

"Good question. We seem to be all right for the moment. No explosions, no one's stopped breathing."

"And … let's keep it that way."

"You want me to turn off the lantern? Look around and get your bearings, Nikki. What are you looking for, and *where* are you looking?"

"I'm looking for anything that gives personal information about the long-ago Homer. Just … anything. A journal would be awesome, but that might be asking too much."

"I made it!" Yumi said, stepping into the center of the room with us.

"You came up the ladder?" Alex asked, surprise in his voice.

"I took the stairs, and see? I'm not broken."

"Yumi," Alex reprimanded, "you must let us know if you're going to do something like that!"

"And be told not to do it? I can be adventuresome too. Anyway, all the steps held me. And only that second one from the top felt a little wobbly. But, still, it held me fine."

"It would be good if Nikki could take the steps down," Alex said. "Getting back on the ladder from the landing is much trickier than coming off it."

"Oh, now you tell me," I whined. "Anyway, let's look for personal paperwork."

"Look at this place," Yumi exclaimed. "Neat as a pin. The bed made, nothing lying about at all."

I'd gone into the kitchen and began rummaging around through the cupboards. "Even more strange, there's nothing here. No food, no hundred-year-old loaf of bread." I opened the little icebox. "Completely empty!"

"There's almost nothing in this little closet. Just this plaid flannel shirt on a hanger I won't touch for fear of it disintegrating."

"Nothing under the bed," Mitch said.

I crossed the apartment to a little desk in the corner of the room that I hadn't seen at first. "There's got to be something here. Would you bring me the lantern, Alex?"

"Sure."

As I sat at the small roll top desk, my three friends came and stood around me. I cautiously started to roll the top of the desk up—it rolled neatly, without stalling, as if it was used to rolling up every day.

"*Yes!*" I whispered, seeing three neat stacks of papers and a little notebook. I pulled off my backpack and got out my gloves. "What have we here?" But I was disappointed. The stacks of papers were only store invoices, and the accompanying notebook was a list of those invoices, neatly input with very tidy handwriting.

"Nothing. Not a thing."

"What about the little drawer underneath?" Mitch asked.

"Oh, I didn't see it!" Hope renewed, I pulled open the drawer, but again, disappointing. It contained a stack of beautiful advertising flyers for the mercantile, and nothing else.

Alex's phone rang. *"Oh-oh!"* He quickly answered it. "Sorry, Dad, time got away from me. I'll be there as soon as I can in about …" I saw him computing how long it would take us to climb down ladders and stairs, walk—*carefully!*—all the way back along the boardwalk to the dirt stairs, up the dirt stairs, stow everything, and then get back to Zingas' grocery. If nothing went the least bit wrong, it would take us at least …. "It'll take me about an hour-and-a-half to get there, Dad."

"Where the hell are you?" everyone heard Mr. Zingas yell. Our eyes grew large. We had never seen nor heard Mr. Zingas angry.

This was decidedly not good.

"I'll be there as soon as I can, Dad." And, adding to my shock, Alex hung up on his father.

"Oh. No." I whispered, closing the desk, looking around to see that everything was in order, not that there was anything there to be out of order. And not that there was anyone to care if it was.

"Not good," Alex said. "I completely forgot I had to get back to the store. Let's get in motion. Mitch, you go down the ladder first and be below to help Yumi and Nikki if they need it. I'll stay up here to help from this end if necessary."

We watched as Mitch negotiated his way under the railing and onto the ladder, I could see what Alex meant about the difficulty. When Mitch touched down on the ground, Yumi stepped onto the landing, and, holding tightly onto the railing made her way down the stairs safely.

I felt a surprising anxiety, starting to follow her. She was easily ten pounds—or more, I didn't want to think about it—lighter than me. What if the stairs would not hold? I grasped the railing, stepped down on the first step, then reached to the third step, deciding to avoid the second altogether. If I were to fall, the closer to the ground the better.

"You're okay, Nikki," Mitch said reassuringly from the ground, but his voice wavered, and I knew he was considerably more afraid for me than he had been for himself.

"Yeah, Nikki, you're doing great," Yumi cheered. But her voice was no more confident than Mitch's. I could feel Alex on the landing above, ready to jump into action, if necessary.

I crept down two more steps. Then I felt safe. Only five more steps. As I came to two steps above ground, Mitch reached out and literally plucked me from the step and held me close.

Oh, wow! Talk about romantic! I could have stayed airborne in his arms for two eternities!

"Stand back," Alex said.

Mitch set my feet on the ground and we stood back, wondering why.

Alex turned and sat on the railing and sped to the ground, right before our very eyes.

"Ohhhh!" Yumi said. "We have us some amazing men!"

"We do. Even if one of them, and by association, all of us, is in big trouble. I think we can leave the ladder where it is."

"*Ack!* I left the ring of skeleton keys on the table," Alex moaned.

"It's okay," I said. "Let's get in motion. We need to move quickly but safely."

"Quickly and safely," Yumi repeated, leading the way through the little, unassuming door, back through the storage room, through the store, and out the front door. Mitch, bringing up the rear, closed the door and we were on our way to sunshine and reprimand.

We made good time through the underground city, becoming increasingly aware of the turns, the caution spots, the darker-than-ever spots, and the smooth-going spots. But we did not come out to sunshine. The sky had broken open, and there was a full-on torrent of rain pummeling us as we poked our heads like little moles out of the ground.

"Let's not bother to stow stuff in the trunk," Mitch suggested. "Let me run out and unlock the car, then you all scurry out."

"Right," Alex agreed. But I could tell he didn't want to chat about anything.

We watched through a veil of pelting rain as Mitch dashed to the car, almost falling on the slick, wet grass. On the way, he tore off his backpack. Then he unlocked the car, threw his backpack in the back seat, jumped in, and started the car. We all dashed after him, and, if not for the serious tone of the moment, would have been giggling like the nut cases we were.

As it was, we had a nearly wordless trip home, with the added fact that Mitch had to pay close attention to the road, the rain was so completely blinding.

When we got to Zingas Grocery, we let Alex out to face his doom alone. It was his request, and we were disinclined to argue.

We were all in trouble now. And had my dad not just said he was proud of me? This was bound to get back to my parents. But, really, I tried to excuse myself, I didn't do anything wrong. And, in any case, I was trying to do a good deed for someone everyone loved.

I was completely innocent.

Yeah, Nikki, I self-talked, leave one of your very best friends out to hang, will you? How awful would it feel if Mr. Zingas didn't like you anymore? What if he thought you were a bad influence on his son?

And potentially even worse, what if he decided that Yumi was not good for his son, and tried to call a halt to their relationship?

How many kinds of bad could this experience turn out to be, and for what?

I did not have one, single, concrete bit of info I needed to help Homer. Not one. For all the adventure, all I learned was that Homer's ancestor built and owned this one mercantile.

My fantasy of being so darn helpful was probably just that. A silly fantasy. It was not my job to get up into other people's lives.

"But," Other Nikki reminded, "You really did help Yumi's mother. You changed their lives for the better. It wouldn't have happened without you."

Yeah. Maybe.

I didn't know, and I couldn't put any more brainpower to it. I was sad. I felt bad. I felt guilty. And, as we pulled into the parking structure, my too-quiet friends made me think they were sharing similar thoughts. Maybe they were mad at me.

Mitch parked the car and we got out, grabbing out wet backpacks and tool bags, we went inside and headed for the elevators.

Homer was in the hall chatting with one of the residents, but when he spotted us, he excused himself and came up to us. "There you are! Mr. Zingas has called me twice, wondering if you were around, or had turned up. It seems Alex was to be at the grocery a couple hours ago. And without a word from any of you, he was frantic. Which makes me frantic.

"You kids have turned me grey, today!"

I didn't know what to say. Everyone was mad at us.

I finally said, "I didn't know Alex had to be at the store hours ago. He hadn't said anything. Did he, Yumi?"

"Yes. He did tell me he had to be at the grocery this afternoon. But he didn't say the exact time. And … we all … time just got away from us."

"I wouldn't have you turn grey on our account," I protested. O.M.G., that sounded so very weak out loud. It had sounded better in my head. I looked at Mitch, surprised at his silence. But then, I realized, it was much worse for him. Because, well, because of Homer being in their apartment a lot lately.

In other words—*Homer. The. Whole. Entire. Reason. We. Were. Late.*

The elevator finally, thankfully, pinged. What took it so long!?! As, heads hanging, we crawled onto the elevator, Mitch said softly, "I'm so very sorry, Homer."

The doors closed, and we three escaped convicts made our silent way to the seventh floor.

Chapter VIII
A Day on My Own

I gave Mitch no argument when we got to my door and he said he thought he'd better go home. I was sad, though to not even get a little kiss. I felt I deserved a little kiss.

But, still ….

I let Yumi and myself into the apartment and we flopped down on the twin sofas without even turning on a light. The rain, beating against the windows, sounded angry, too. I'd come to love the sound of the rain on the windows. But now, no.

"Hungry?" I asked.

"No. Not really."

"Me neither." We listened to the rain for a minute. "It'll be all right," I said, trying to sound reassuring.

"Really, Nikki? Are you sure?" she said with just a hint of accusation in her soft voice.

Oh! Yumi was angry with me too! This was not fair. *Really not fair.* She could have said something at any minute, like, "I think we need to go back," or even, "I don't want to go." If she hadn't gone, Alex probably wouldn't have gone. It would have been only Mitch and me and everything would have been fine.

Everything would have been fine! Yumi and Alex could have had their day together, doing whatever they pleased, and Mitch and I would have been fine. Thinking over the entire experience, the only time either one of them was the least bit helpful was when Alex climbed the ladder. No, not even then, because Mitch *did* climb the ladder.

I'd come into the apartment feeling terrible and guilty. But now I'd worked myself up into a place of anger. I felt completely disempowered. I got up and went to my room, closing the door with an audible click, then moved to stand by my long, sad windows, watching the rain beat against the glass—the rain streaking down the glass looked like tears. I tried to get that image out of my mind. I looked at the trees below, which I could barely see through the pounding rain, feeling like I might join my windows in their crying.

And then I realized I was crying. I didn't even know it until this great sob came out of me. Everyone hated me! A horrible, horrible feeling overcame me. It wasn't fair. Altogether unfair. I only wanted to do a good thing for a good person. And now, Alex was in trouble, Mitch was distressed about Homer, Yumi feared a rift in her love relationship. Homer was disappointed in me. Someone, for sure, would say something to my parents, and they could be added to the list of "people angry with and disappointed in Nikki."

All because I wanted to be helpful. Why couldn't I figure out how to be selfish like all the people who never seemed to get into trouble, just living their lives with their own personal interests?

And, I decided, that was just what I was going to do from this moment forward. Think about what Nikki wants, and do what Nikki pleases. I felt cold, and then realized I was still wet from the run to the car in the rain. I hadn't even noticed. I went to the closet to dig out my fluffy winter flannel pajamas. I wanted to crawl into bed, curl up into a fetal position, and make the world go away. Maybe I would leave here and go be with my parents. Maybe that's what I needed to do. Maybe I just simply was not mature enough to be on my own. Maybe ….

The maybes stopped in their tracks. The angel in the mirror shined brightly as if waiting for me to come into the closet.

"*No!*" I said, backing out of the closet. "I'm done. I'm not helping anyone, anymore! It's not worth it. I keep getting into trouble."

I stood in my room, hand on the handle of the closet door, completely confused. Yumi's mother had talked with me about the challenges of second sight, and her words came to me now: "It's not easy having second sight. But you have a calling. You'll often know things other people do not know. And, because you love them, you'll want to help them. Because you'll know things they don't know, you may be teased, abused, ignored. But, Nikki, it's your calling. You'll never be able to ignore it, no matter how hard you try."

This from someone who had considerably more experience with "second sight," or whatever this plague was called, than I had. When she said it, I didn't pay much attention to how accurate and wise she was. But I replayed it now with close attention.

So, 1: I would likely always know things other people did not know, 2: I would be inclined to try to help them with this knowledge, and 3: they were likely to not be appreciative.

There was no getting around it. Apprehension tinged with resignation, I opened the closet door and stood before the angel, who waited patiently. I didn't know if he could see me, but I shrugged like, Sorry! I had second thoughts colliding headlong with my second sight. I'm here now.

The light around the angel swirled and out of the turbid roiling appeared the little apartment above the mercantile I had just come from. Except it was bright daylight, and everything was utterly charming. The sun poured in through the little window, showing the neatly made bed, the dining room table with a bunch of cheerful daisies in a vase in the center on a pure white crocheted doily. In the corner stood the desk I had recently pored through. Off to the side, I could see the little kitchen, clean and sparkling.

Altogether enchanting! But, why was I here?

As if in answer to my unspoken question, I was whirled about and brought right up to the little dormer window. I looked out the window, only to see nothing but a wall of light. Totally disappointing, as I hoped to see the street with horses and carriages, and people dressed in their Victorian finery.

But only a wall of light met my gaze.

Out of the corner of my eye, I saw a picture. I turned to look at a sweet watercolor of a little boy lying on his back under a tree by a lake, arms folded behind his head, contemplating the clouds floating overhead, one of which looked very much like a puppy.

It made me grin. But it also made me pay close attention to the picture and the wall it hung on. Yes! I was being shown that behind that picture I would find what I had hoped to find when I was there, earlier today.

Was it really only today? Goodness, what a long and entirely too eventful this one day had been!

The adorable Victorian watercolor of the little boy began to fade, and then the entire charming, sunlit apartment faded from view, and, before long, I stood looking at a vague reflection of myself in the dark closet.

I flipped on the light and dug out my fluffy pjs, took a long hot shower, and soon curled up in bed, warm and cozy, and in a much better frame of mind than I'd been in earlier. If everyone had to be angry with me, they had to deal with it on their own. I wasn't going to feel guilty for intending to be kind and helpful.

The thought crossed my mind as I drifted into sleep that everyone had an opportunity to learn their own lessons in this situation. I was only responsible for my own.

*   *

When I woke up in the morning replaying the events of the previous day, I discovered that I had no desire to be around anyone today. I wasn't angry, I wasn't, *thank goodness!*, sad. And an even bigger thank goodness! was that I didn't feel guilty.

I just … needed to be alone. It was only six-thirty and very unlikely that Yumi would be up yet. So I slipped into jeans and a teeshirt, grabbed up my damp backpack on the way through the living room, tiptoed out to the kitchen, and threw together a couple PB and Js, grabbed a couple bottles of fruit juice, stuck them in my backpack, dug out the car keys from the little table by the door, picked up the damp tool bag, and slipped out, scurrying down the hall to the elevators.

On the ground floor, I cautiously stuck my head out, hoping to not see Homer, or anyone for that matter. Coast clear, I zipped across to the door to the parking structure and out to my folks' car. Now was the moment I felt gratitude that I'd had the weird, insistent foresight to get my driver's license the day after Yumi's mother went back to Southern California.

I started the engine, got out my phone, and texted my three friends: "Need a day alone. Phone off. See you later."

I hoped that sounded like I felt. Not mad. Not sad. Not guilty. Just, simply needing some autonomous space.

All. By. Myself. "It's good to be by oneself on occasion," I told the rearview mirror.

The day was sparkling and brilliant, everything translucent-looking after the torrential rain. This was something I had come to understand and love about Seattle. The rain I thought I hated was what made it the Emerald City. The rain I had come to love. The rain that made one contemplative, introspective, followed by brilliant, translucent clarity. Boy, I was thinking up a philosophical storm!

I rolled down the windows and let the cool, brisk, early-morning breeze pour through the car. Out with the stale air, in with the fresh. It was also delightful that I now knew the road to the underground city like the back of my hand, and didn't have to concentrate so hard on where to turn, leaving me free to revisit the stunning vision I'd had last night. Goodness! I was beginning to take these super-normal paranormal events as if they were everyday occurrences.

Which they are not!

Just the appearance of the angel alone would make anyone change their ways, if their ways needed changing.

The familiar little hillside finally came into view. I pulled up onto it, gathered my backpack and tools and headed down the dirt steps. I paused, of course, under Millie's lovely face looking up at the sky. "I need you and the angel to watch over me, Millie. I know I'll be fine, but doubly so with your protection."

I stepped down into the darkness, put on my headlamp, turned it on and adjusted it, then turned on my flashlight, and headed into the darkness. I passed the "Mitch and I Learn we have Feelings for Each Other" porch, then eventually passed Yumi's so many Greats Aunt's house, and then found myself in much less familiar terrain. Bits of greenish-bluish phosphorescence glowed in the earthen walls, and the occasional sound of a drip of water reverberated. I hadn't noticed that before, and I guessed it was because I'd not been alone, and we were either chatting, or just the sound of our footsteps covered the dripping water.

To be honest, it *was* a bit unnerving. But I'd come a long ways, in both the underground city and in my life, since the first time I came down here alone looking for Mitch, ever so long ago now, it seemed.

I crept along slowly, flashing my light from my feet to the boardwalk ahead, back and forth. I had that uncomfortable feeling of the mercantile being much farther than I expected, just like I had before, and I reminded myself that this is how I felt yesterday, even with friends with me, so there was nothing to worry about. It's not like the mercantile disappeared overnight, I chided my ever-more-uncomfortable self.

"You can turn around," I said aloud. "*Around-around*," echoed off the walls. "Oh!" "*oh-oh!*" came back. I *definitely* did not notice this echo yesterday. "No!" I whispered. I've come this far and *no turning back*, silly-chicken-girl! I said much more quietly.

And then what happened? The mercantile popped up when I was prepared to go some distance yet! Grinning at no one, I walked up the little incline and up the steps to the front door, and walked into the mercantile like I owned the place. Well, I didn't, but technically, my two friends, Yumi and Mitch, did.

I went through the store, into the storage room, stopping at the foot of the angel, who still looked through me like I was of no consequence.

But I knew better! The energy of the angel and I were on the same paranormal wavelength, the cold-stone artifact did not need to give me warm-fuzzies.

I grabbed a rope on the way through the storage room and went out the unassuming little door. With a sense of purpose and no hesitation, I took my backpack off, tied one end of the rope to it, tied the other to the tool bag, and placed the tool bag on the highest step I could reach. Then I clung to the metal pipe railing as I cautiously stepped on the first step—after all, these two bottom steps I'd not stepped on the day before, as Mitch reached out and grabbed me.

Again—*wow! romantic!*

Returning my attention to the potentially dangerous task at hand, I stepped onto the next step, and the next, and continued up the steps, stepping over the second from the top step. I breathed a sigh of relief as I touched down on the stairway landing. Then I went through the unlocked door and turned to pull my tool bag from the stairs up to me.

"*Ta-da!*" I crowed, feeling pretty darn pleased with myself. I didn't need anyone. I could do this all by myself. I didn't need to get others into trouble, or mad at me, or any of that! "*Nikki, aka, Wonder Woman!*" I crowed some more. A girl with a mission needed a moment for self-kudos, and this was mine.

Then—back to the mission. I crossed the little apartment, my two little battery-operated lights very poor imitation of the beautiful sunlit space I'd seen in the vision. But that vision stuck in my head, and it was almost as if it super-imposed upon the current darkness. I felt a pang of pity that the adorable mercantile was not out in the sunshine and rain, enjoying life like every other mercantile in the world.

I stood in the window dormer, looking down at the blackness, where the boardwalk passed by, imagining people coming and going to and from what must have been one of their favorites stores, with all the wonderful and charming Victorian goodies and useful items held within. I then noticed that I seemed to be avoiding the reason I came here, both relishing the moment on one hand, and a fear on the other, that what I sought I would not find.

I turned, and, with a sigh of relief, saw the watercolor painting, the little boy looking at the same puppy cloud he had looked at for generations. The thought threatened to overtake my mind, and I had to set it aside, along with the painting. I took it down from the wall and put it carefully on the floor. And there, conspicuously, was a little wooden door built into the wall, with a latch. There wasn't even a lock.

I turned the little latch, and behind the door sat a black-covered, thin book with "Journal" stamped in silver lettering on its cover.

Yes! This is the treasure for which you seek I thought, taking the journal to the dining room table and opening it to the first page ….

Chapter IX
Ḩomer Ḿuller's Journal
February 1, 1882

Dear Journal – today we begin our journey together. I guess most people write in a journal to recap their day, and whatever thoughts they have about that day. But this journal has only one purpose, and that's to record what I find out— and I do hope this journal has some significant entries—about my real family, and who I really am.

So, Journal, I'll start from what I know for a fact. I'm Romanian.

I came to the great-and-terrible city of New York with my family in approximately the Year-of-Our-Lord 1859.

I say approximately because I don't know for sure. I was, I believe, five-years-old. Also, an approximation. I got separated from my family when we debarked. I remember I had a lot of siblings, several older and a little sister—I was to hang onto her hand, as she hung onto our father's hand. I believe there was a baby my mother was holding.

I remember such a crush of people as I'd never known was possible. And I remember my sister's hand being pulled from mine. Everything after that was so horrible, for so long. They all spoke a language I didn't know. They had me in a terrible place, and then I was taken to another terrible place, which was the orphanage, where I was to spend the next ten years of my life until I ran away, and made my escape to Seattle.

I'd heard about Seattle, and I saw a picture of it somewhere, and, even though the picture was black and white, I could just tell it was green, and that seemed like my childhood home before we left.

Why did my parents take their many children across a great ocean to land in, what was for me, the horrors of New York, leaving behind a beautiful country? A belief in a better life, a promise of financial security, I suppose.

July 1, 1882

Hello, Journal—I'm back. My apologies for my absence. I have a wonderful mercantile that I've built almost single-handedly. I worked hard to gather some money together, and have been a good customer to other businesses, and so have been able to acquire credit from my bank to start my business. The building is nearly done. I've been living in a tent on the premises. When I get my little apartment put together on the second floor of my store, I'll feel like a king, looking out my little window on the world of Seattle!

I spent some time in the library today. Again, about my main subject, Journal, for writing in you. I was looking for any records that might be there, that would lead to information about my family.

A charming librarian listened to my verbal sketch of my story. She acted as though my story touched her, which certainly must only be professionally appropriate behavior. Why would she care about me? A sad little foreign orphan. But it felt both wonderful and frightening, dear Journal, to whisper—because I was in the library—some of the details of my life, and what I was hoping to find in the library.

She showed me certain volumes that might have information I could use in my search, and then she showed me the newspapers the library gets. Imagine! Getting newspapers from New York and Chicago and Denver and Minneapolis and even Dallas! Although, of course, they were days late, it was wonderful to see what was happening in other cities.

"You never know," the librarian said, "some little article in a newspaper could lead to information that leads to information that leads to the very thing you search."

Again, very sweet of her. Well, they also keep newspapers, back for decades. It's truly remarkable, really. Who knows? I might find out who my family is, and if I have any living relatives. With so many children in the family, there's bound to be someone.

Will they want to see me? That remains to be seen.

But I want to see them, Journal!

October 12, 1882

The store is almost built. I've been working very hard, and with the help of a couple men with strong building skills, it's looking as beautiful as I'd hoped. I've taken down my tent and moved my cot inside, among all the sawdust and boards. Not like a home yet, but the wood smells wonderful, and my future of serving the community does now seem like a true possibility!

March 31, 1883

My apologies, again, Journal for the lapse in entries. Building and putting together the mercantile and, even more importantly, my comfortable second story home where I am now writing from my beautiful little desk, has taken all my time and attention—including my mission of finding my people. I will be back upon that soon, as never a day passes that I don't wonder if I have family alive.

August 20, 1883

Again, Journal, months of lapse in time. But, oh so much to tell! Miss Sumner, the librarian, yes, I address her by name now we have become that familiar, has turned up wonderful information—the roster to the ship that I very likely came to the United States on. I now have a list of names of people from Romania, one of which is very likely my real name!

Miss Sumner is amazing and has done surprising research on my behalf. I don't know why. I even asked her. She said my story has touched her, and she has time, in her job, to do research. Well, I'm grateful, and I guess if the God of All cares to take a glance at me with this remarkable gift of a librarian who has the talent and time to help me find my people, then all I can say is I'm filled with gratitude. I send prayers of thanks to the heavens.

November 17, 1883

Great news, Journal! I've been learning things about the people on the list of names from the ship's roster. The Albescu are stonemasons, and not just ordinary stonemasons, but talented stone carvers. They have a catalog which I have waited with breathless anticipation to come. It came today, *and they have angels!*

You know, Journal, my affinity for angels, messengers of God, and comforters of the human family. I am sending a wire to order one in the morning. Even though a wire is expensive, I cannot wait! My angel is ten-feet tall and has an amazing face. I don't care about the expense of the marble angel, either, nor even the question Miss Sumner posed about where I'll put it. As she's the person who found the family name for me, I shared with her the catalog and my intentions of procuring the largest angel they offer.

As I say, I don't care where I'll put it. It means so much to me to have it. Carved by an artisan from my homeland, and maybe even someone I'm related to!

April 5, 1884

So much happening in my life, Journal, and it is all wonderful. Today the angel ….

My flashlight flickered! I had become so engrossed in Victorian Homer's life, that I completely forgot that I was in the underground city with only my flashlight and headlight for light! Terror struck me as I thought of being here in total darkness. I would not be the least bit able to get out!

I threw the journal into my backpack, hurried out the door, let my tool bag down to the ground with a *plop!,* closed the door to the apartment, and quickly hurried down the stairs, stepping over the second from the top, holding on with all my might to the railing. I grabbed up the tool bag, untied the rope, and let it drop where I stood, then made my way back through the storage room, through the store and out the front, my flashlight flickering and becoming weaker all the way.

I stepped onto the boardwalk, peering into the darkness, flashlight dimming, while, thankfully, my headlamp continued shining brightly. Be calm, I told myself, just take it one step at a time, you'll soon be in more familiar territory.

As I stepped cautiously but with urgency, the relieving thought came to mind that my phone had a bright flashlight, that I never used and wasn't exactly sure how to make it come on. I debated whether I should stop and get it out, or just keep moving. I opted to keep moving while, if I could, get my phone out.

I realized I had to set the tool bag down and retrieve it another time. I needed my hands! I took in a landmark for the tool bag, setting it in the middle of the boardwalk so it would not be missed the next time any of us were down here. As I crept along, I pulled my backpack off, zipped it open and rummaged for my phone.

I couldn't find it. And then it hit me, it was not in my backpack, it was on the car seat, where I left it after turning it off.

Truly terrified now, with my headlamp dimming, I hurried, praying, please, please, let me get to light! I came to Yumi's ancestor aunt's house. Wonderful! I was now familiar with the area, although, of course, I could not see the boardwalk if it became completely dark.

As if the terrible fates read my mind, the headlamp blinked out. Shocked by the total darkness, I didn't even cry out, or make a sound. Shocked! I sat down on the boardwalk, berating myself for sitting in the little apartment, reading the journal as if I had all the time in the world to do just that.

What was the matter with me? Sometimes my thinking was deranged. Oh, the total black darkness was terrible. *Terrible.* I thought about what it might take to be found. Would my friends come here looking for me? How long would that take?

But as I sat, I was surprised to see the faintest of light. Yes! Light! As my eyes adjusted to the darkness, the light from the stairs, some distance yet ahead, barely reached me. I would crawl, first one hand and then the next, feeling the boardwalk, tiny increment by tiny increment.

And so I began my baby-crawl, one hand, one knee, the other hand, the other knee, inch by inch, until I began to even make out some forms of the houses around me. Now I actually did start to cry, I was so relieved!

"Stop blubbering, Nikki," I reprimanded. "You're blurring your vision." Right, I thought, just remain calm, and keep moving.

And, wonder of wonders, I began to see actual light. Real sunshine from the dirt stairwell. I still couldn't make out the boardwalk, black against black. But I knew I would make it, bruised knees and all. And before long, I saw the stairwell, beckoning to me like a lighthouse—here is a safe haven.

I probably could have stood at that point, but I continued to crawl, right to the bottom step, which, with a flood of gratitude I could not possibly name, I sat upon.

I was shaking, my knees hurt, and, looking at my palms, I was shocked to see that my left palm was bleeding. I couldn't even feel the pain, I was so overrun with adrenalin. I had a two-inch wood sliver in my palm. *I couldn't even feel it!* And still, I was shaking so badly, I couldn't get a proper hold on it.

I took my dead headlight off and stuck it in my backpack, then sat, quieting myself until I stopped shaking and my breathing returned to something resembling normal. Finally, I gathered myself, climbed up the steps into the glorious sunshine, and made my way to the car. Unlocking the door, I threw the jacket covering my phone aside. Yes, there it was, mocking me … "You think you're so independent!"

"You know what, little phone," I said, "I am independent. I didn't make the smartest choices, but I worked it out as I went along. So, yeah, I do think I'm independent!" I waved my arms around for emphasis, and my left hand bumped into the car door frame.

"OUCH!" I yelped, having forgotten the mega-sliver. "Yes, an example of my less than brilliant moves."

I then took the time to extricate the sliver, which, fortunately, came out readily, all in one piece, without, it appeared, any fragments remaining. I'd have to remember to give it a good disinfecting when I got home.

Now, I asked myself, are you ready to go home?

No, I answered. I needed to get back to ancestor Homer's story. I wasn't ready to plunge into my own life, as I remained utterly engaged in his.

I retrieved the journal from my backpack, with the passing thought that, now that I have my phone's light, I could go back and get my tool bag. But, no, I wasn't that brave. I got out of the car and found a comfortable spot on the ground, next to a gigantic rock, and settled in.

Now, where was I?

April 5, 1884

So much happening in my life, Journal, and it is all wonderful. Today the angel arrived! It was quite a production to get it to the store, and with so much attention. My assistant and I picked it up at the train station. It was crated up, but I wanted to make sure it had made the journey without damage, so my assistant and I uncrated him. The more we exposed of the magnificent marble carving, the bigger the crowd that gathered.

I felt very shy about the attention and just wanted to get the angel home. But even on the road, everyone stopped and stared at the angel that just barely fit in the cart. Finally, we came to the back of the mercantile, and then it was not much to slide it down a ramp. The two of us walked the angel into the storage area. I had my assistant open the store back up, while I sat in a chair under the angel's gaze, contemplating the wonder of it.

There's more to tell, Journal. But I must go to sleep now.

November 25, 1884

Dear Journal, you will not believe what I'm about to write. Yes, I know, look at the expanse of time that has passed. But what has occurred in that time? That's the question that intrigues. And I'm about to share the most incredible news I would never have imagined I would write.

I've been keeping a secret from you, Journal, and that is that Miss Adelaide Sumner and I have developed a lovely friendship. Much to my surprise, she told me that her interest in researching my family was not only a professional engagement, but that she'd been drawn to me from the first time we chatted, whispering in the beautiful library among the wise old books.

As it happens, we share many interests. I won't go into all that right now because, what has transpired, dimming everything else in my life, I still can't believe.

I don't know what possessed me, or where the courage came from, but I dared to ask her, last evening, as I walked her home from the library when she got off work as I often do, if she could imagine a life with me.

And she said, Oh, I will never forget her words, the sound of her voice, the light in her eyes when she said, "Mr. Muller, what, in heavens name has taken you so long!"

And, Journal, my patient, discreet friend, I further gathered my courage to ask her if she would be willing to consider becoming my wife.

The result? I am now betrothed to a brilliant and beautiful living, breathing, angel. How is this possible?

I am filled with gratitude.

May 9, 1885

Can you fill in the great expanse of blanks, dear Journal? Addie and I, my endearment for my beloved, set a date for our wedding, which put me fast upon building a little home of our own. It will be finished this week, whereupon all the furniture and charming bric-a-brac we've been buying that's in the storage room gets to come out, and we will have a wonderful time putting things in place, just in time for our wedding, two weeks hence. In case you don't hear from me again before then, Journal, we will afterward take a lovely trip for a few days to Victoria, B.C.

Researching my family line has become less compelling in the light of making a family of my own. Although, perhaps, one day, it will become important to me again.

May 30, 1886

Yes Journal, a year. A wonderful, love-filled, and business-successful year. It seems that, Journal, you've become a repository for brief comments about my greatest news. And here's the news that outshines all other news, even the marriage. Not only did I never imagine that anyone would fall in love with this humble orphan, but someone incredible did! Even more, I could never imagine that I would be a father. But I soon will be!

Me, little orphan Homer, now, about to become a father.

Thank you to all the miraculous powers in the universe! I am humbled. I can say no more.

June 4, 1889

Hello Journal! Perhaps you don't even remember me. But I do have something so very important to share. Our beautiful son, which Addie insisted on naming Homer, poor thing—I would have called him something else, but she was firm on the matter—anyway, our son is now nearing three years of age, and, much to my surprise, the nagging feeling about my family has returned. It's different now, though, because I want to know for my son's sake. I want to know anything about my heritage because it is also *his* heritage.

I hadn't said anything, but Addie, brilliant woman that she is! reads me like an open book.

Which, I suppose is appropriate for a librarian. She has insisted that I take a trip to New York to find my people and to learn whatever I can. She has continued to do her research on my behalf, and she handed me a detailed list of where to go, who to ask for, and even notes about what I might find from that source.

I'm quite torn. I don't desire to leave my little family, while, at the same time, I need to learn what I can. So I'll go to New York. I'm leaving on the train this afternoon. I look forward to the next time I have something to share with you, Journal. It seems always to be exciting and wonderful.

Chapter X
Information Conduit

I sat staring at the date of the last entry. *It was two days before the Great Seattle Fire.*

What had happened to Homer and his family? Did he go to New York? Would he have heard about the fire as he journeyed across the continent? Did he hurry back home? The store is intact, so it was either rebuilt or unharmed when the city decided to rebuild on top of the previous city, to get away from all the problems of the water being higher than the land.

I couldn't help feeling completely overwhelmed by Homer's story. Whatever happened, time had passed them all by as their stories fell away into history.

But, still, there was the current Homer, whose life story and love story was unfolding, this very minute. So interesting that both Homers had similar stories! Did I hold the key to help solve Homer's dilemma?

It really didn't seem like it, because, with all the touching story in the ancestor Homer's journal, the question: "Who am I?" had not been answered.

Was the artist who carved the marble angel an actual relative of Homer's? Was Homer and his family on the ship that Addie had found the roster for? Was Mitch's mother's ancestors on that same ship? And, the most burning question of all, was Homer's family and Mitch's family the same family?

How was I to find out more? The angel brought me to this journal. And it has some answers–but not the *big* answers. Then the obvious next step came to mind. Go to the *above-ground* Seattle library and continue my sleuthing. I now had, in Homer's journal, dates and a few names.

As I closed the journal, thumbing through the last few blank pages again just to be sure I didn't miss anything, I discovered that I *had* missed something—the journal had a pocket inside the back cover! I slid out a piece of paper I found there, and, to my surprise, unfolded a copy of a ship's roster.

I jumped up and ran to the car. Now I really had something, and it was my turn to find a brilliant, caring librarian, who could hopefully move this mystery to the next level.

*   *

I didn't even turn on my phone. I knew there'd be a raft of messages and calls, and I could not have my focus disrupted. As I drove back toward the city, I recalled the only time I'd been in the main library, with Dad when he had to get a photocopy of some rare document that had something to do with his job.

Now I *did* have to turn on my phone to get directions to the library, and I stoically ignored everything but communication with my GPS. As I drove, I went over what I needed to asked the librarian so I wouldn't sound stupid, and so I wouldn't get derailed by the "shiny object" syndrome—because there were possibly many things that could come up that I would find fascinating, but would it have to do with the subject?

As I came into town, the amazing, eleven-story structure of the downtown library overtook my thoughts—one kinda has to see it to believe it—and wended my way into its underground parking.

I put the journal and my phone in my backpack and started to jump out when I realized I had to think about being asked where I got the journal. Where did I get the ship's roster? I decided I wouldn't show the journal, but I could say I found the roster in a very old book I bought at a second-hand shop. Or some-such.

Not a deep-dark lie, which I've never been able to pull off, but a sort of pinkish-white lie. Because the intention was good, made of kindness.

I made my way from the parking lot up to the main desk. I pulled my backpack off, got out the journal, and gently removed the ship's roster from the envelope in the back of the journal.

"May I help you?" a kindly, middle-aged librarian wearing a lacy white blouse, asked in a subdued voice.

"Yes," I whispered back, carefully unfolding the roster. "I'm wondering how much information might possibly be gleaned from this one document about someone's ancestors?"

"May I?" she asked, gesturing to the roster.

I nodded, turning the document to face her.

"Oh! Interesting!" she said. "Ship's Roster of the S.S. Bucharest, June 5, 1855." She looked up at me, smiling. "How did you come across such a document, dear? It's most interesting."

"Well, I found it … ahm, rummaging around in the back of a closet." Sort of true. I found it because of the scrying mirror in my closet.

"What a find! And you're wondering if, coincidently, it has something to do with the ancestors of someone you know?"

"*Hmmmm…*" I mused. Far-fetched, at a minimum, she was right. But, I couldn't fabricate beyond this point. Not much, anyway, because we could rapidly get into territory where I didn't find out anything that I needed to know for Homer's sake. "A bit strange, I know, but, yes, as it happens, yes. I tend to, ah, have things happen around me that are a bit … unusual."

The kindly librarian inclined her head slightly in acknowledgment. "It happens. You are what I call 'a serendipity.'"

"A serendipity?"

"Yes. A person who is a conduit of generally assumed unknowable information. I encounter it far too often to say it does not exist. But!" And she bent her head to the roster, "tell me what it is you're looking for, and we'll sleuth it out. You know, the library system has gathered considerable amounts of information over the years, so much is now available that was not before."

A serendipity! I thought. A person who is like a conduit of information for other people. That was me, for sure. "I have a friend who has wondered who his ancestors might be. It has recently become more important to him. He told me that his great-great, maybe three greats, uncle came over on a ship with his family, and, probably other families, around this date," I pointed to the roster.

"Then, unhappily, the little boy, my friend's ancestor uncle, got separated from his family. As he spoke no English, and, there was such a crush of people, the sad story is that he ended up in an orphanage. And then, I guess, as soon as he could, he ran away and came across the continent as a young teenager, and ended up doing quite well for himself, here in Seattle.

"He built a mercantile that was doing well, but, because of the question of who his family might be, and wondering if he had any living relatives, he decided to return to New York for a while to see what he might find.

"And that's pretty much where the story ends. My friend is following his Great-Uncle's path, wondering about who his ancestors might be. When I turned up this roster, I thought it might be possible that it is the one his ancestors are listed on. And, although it sounds strange, this sort of thing happens to me, and as you say, I may be a "serendipity'—which, by the way, I love. Thank you."

"You're welcome, dear. Okay, let's see what we can find out. Follow me."

I followed her to another section of the library where there was a row of computers. She gestured for me to join her as she sat before one of them. "Is there any more information you can give me?"

"I don't think so. My friend's name is Homer Muller, but, of course, that has nothing to do with anything, as, I guess, the orphanage gave him a name. That name isn't on the roster, and I think, if they'd had his name, they probably would have found his family."

"Well, maybe. It wasn't as easy then to do such a thing as it would be now. Lots of immigrants, speaking their own language, coming to the states with stars in their eyes, not fully aware of what their lives were likely to be like. But I applaud their intrepid persistence. This country is built on diversity. We need to remember that.

"Enough preaching, especially to, I believe, the choir," she said, chuckling softly.

"Yes, pretty much," I agreed.

"So, we're looking for any sort of record about a missing Romanian boy child from this particular ship's roster. Let me read the list over and see if anything triggers a thought. You're lucky to be talking with me, as I have a particular interest in Seattle's Victorian era."

"From what you say, I'm serendipitous. So it's no accident I've met you."

"Yes. You're right! Serendip …." She paused. "Oh, ho, look here. This is interesting! A family with the surname Radu came over on this ship."

"Yes?"

"Well, they historically did quite a lot to build this city. The Radus married into the Eder family, and in the early 1900s were very active in building Seattle after the Great Fire.

"Wait a minute! The Radus?" I said, stunned. I had seen these letters on a cross-stitch wall hanging in Mitch's kitchen. Was this Mitch's mom's maiden name?

"Is that meaningful?"

"Maybe. My neighbor has a wall hanging with those letters on it. It looks antique and like cross-stitch. It's a saying, I guess, in Romanian. I can't read it, but these letters are across the bottom."

"Oh! It's called a sampler. Fascinating! Well, let's see if we can find this little lost boy."

"Yes. Let's!" I felt a bit overwhelmed by this unanticipated large chunk of information falling into my lap, entirely … unanticipatedly. It could certainly turn out that Mitch's mom's ancestors were the family who had lost their little boy.

"Let's pull up any New York Romanian newspapers, or communications among that population, and see if there's anything there."

I could say nothing but waited in growing anticipation as the librarian thrashed through piles of information that made my head spin. "It's really amazing how fairly any document that has survived into recent times has been input and is available … ah, here we are!"

She pulled up a document with lettering similar to that on the cross-stitch in Mitch's kitchen.

"Now, let's translate it into English, as my Romanian is a bit rusty."

"You speak Romanian?"

"Just a very little bit."

The librarian continued to augment my boundless awe of her. An unassuming-white-lace-blouse-wearing-grey-haired-glasses-embellished demigod of brilliance. I watched as the letters before me turned into ones considerably more familiar.

"If we're fortunate, or, excuse me, serendipitous, there'll be something here." She spun through the pages making my head spin. She obviously knew what she was looking for.

"And here it is!" she exclaimed. *"Oops!"* she whispered. "I'm getting carried away with the moment. Look here." She pointed to where she was reading, "'The Sandu family continues to grieve the loss of their 5-year-old son, Homer, having become separated from the family when they debarked from the S.S. Bucharest, two years ago. We ask again if anyone has the least possible lead or bit of information regarding the whereabouts of their son, please do not hesitate to notify the paper's editor, or the family directly,' followed by addresses."

She sat back with a satisfied sigh. "There's your lost little boy, named Homer Sandu."

"Wow," I said. "That's my friend's first name, Homer."

"Well, although he didn't speak English, he probably was able to communicate his name."

"Right, that makes sense." Puzzled, I tried to imagine what it would be like to have a child simply disappear from your hands. It must have been so very terrible. "But … why, *why* didn't they go to the orphanages looking for him?"

"Good question, by the way, what's your name, dear?"

"Nikki. Nikki Francis."

"Very pleased to meet you, Nikki. I'm Elvira." We shook hands and both sort of giggled because we'd been talking and only now introduced ourselves.

"Wonderful to meet you, Elvira. You're amazing! But, yeah, why didn't they go to the orphanage to find Homer?"

"It's hard to say. They were immigrants. They were trying to sort out their life here. They had other children. Life was not easy. Leaving their community meant going into a world of a different language, a different culture, with accompanying prejudice. It's sad. One has to imagine that it happened more than this one time. But this time, it turned out well. Homer, obviously extremely bright and resourceful, made his way across the continent, as, you've said, a young teenager. Bravo Homer! And made a good life for himself here.

"And now you can tell his great-however many greats-nephew his true last name."

"And the maiden name of my neighbor is most likely Radu, and her ancestors were on the same ship."

"It definitely appears as though that is the case." Elvira folded up the ship's roster and handed it to me. "This was a fun mystery!"

"Amazing, truly, amazing. Yes, a fun mystery. And one day, I'm likely to come back in and tell you the follow-up of today's revelations."

"Well! I would truly like that, my friendly young sleuth."

I grinned. "Do you suppose I could have a copy of that news story, and this other information you've come up with?"

"Of course." She pushed a couple buttons, and soon, out popped Homer's History, and she handed them to me.

I took the papers and stood, giving her a little wave. "Thanks ever so much, Elvira!"

"You're most welcome, dear."

I hurried out to my car, grinning all the way. What profound, incredible success, and all in just one day! A *loooong* day, but still, only one day. As I turned on the engine, Mitch's ring came on my phone.

"Hi!" I answered, filled with the super-joy of the moment.

"*Where are you!?!*" He said in an accusing, angry tone of voice I'd never heard. "Alex and I are here, standing over your tool bag."

They were in the underground city, looking for me.

"Oh, no! I … I'm at the library."

"We were just at the library, and the mercantile, and you're nowhere to be found."

"No. The downtown library. The main library. The library above ground. You won't believe what I've discovered."

"What you've discovered, Nikki? What I don't believe is that you would put everyone what you've put us through today."

"Wait a minute! Wait a minute, Mitch! I texted you and everyone. I said I needed some time to myself. Yes, even you. I was not in the mood to be blasted for trying to do a good deed. Are you telling me I can't have some time to myself?"

"Some time to yourself. Fine. But you disappeared for the whole day."

"Well, Mitch, I'm truly sorry if I caused you distress, and I apologize. I can do no more than that. I'm in my car, heading home. You can berate me there if you must." I disconnected without even saying good-bye. Oh, so, I felt angry, too! Was that right? No. I shouldn't be angry with Mitch because I frightened him.

I pulled out of the parking space and headed in the direction of home. I would make it up to him. I would apologize some more. I would get calm and not be angry because someone cared about me.

Come on, Nikki, be smart! I advised. Mitch is the best part of your life. Yes. You've messed up by being gone all day. I looked at my watch. Five-thirty p.m. I'd been gone almost twelve hours....

But what a twelve hours!

Chapter XI
Everything Goes Wrong

As I drove home, I felt crazy-proud of myself. In my mind, I organized my game plan. I'd go up to the apartment, input my notes and print them out so that they were nice and neat, scan in the documents Elvira had just given me, ad put all the papers in a new folder, and, somewhat ceremoniously, hand it to Homer when I could get him alone for a few moments. I didn't want anyone else to be around when I gave him this information, because I knew *he* wouldn't want anyone else around.

And then, he could do as he pleased with the information. Whether he advanced his relationship with Mitch's mom or not was none of my business.

But, of course, the cupid in me sincerely hoped he would. How romantic! They did seem like the perfect couple. It might be a little bit weird for Mitch to have Homer as a stepdad, but that was a small thing as compared with two people finding one another.

Just like Mitch and I have found each other. And Yumi and Alex.

But then, *ohhhh!* I remembered how angry Mr. Zingas was with us yesterday. Goodness! Was it only yesterday?

Arg! All this anger swirling around, a veritable hurricane of anger swirling around me. But I was about to fix it all, wasn't I? I had to be the calm eye of the storm, doing what I knew best to do.

I could do no more.

As I pulled into the apartment's parking structure, I took a couple deep breaths, centering myself. I would scurry in, hoping to see no one, and once in the apartment, put *Homer's History* folder together. I assumed Yumi to be with Mitch and Alex, so I could do this without interruption, and go find Homer before my three friends got home.

I scurried in, but I was not to be unnoticed. Homer stood in front of the elevators, a disgruntled and extremely unfamiliar look on his face.

"There you are! Miss Francis, you have caused me an undue amount of anxiety, and even risking my job." He came to me and opened the door to the parking structure and ushered me back out into the parking lot. "To say I'm disappointed in you is an understatement. For some reason, everyone expects me to be your babysitter, everyone comes to me about where the dickens you are. Really, I cannot be doing this. I could get in big trouble with how everyone is going on around me."

"But, Homer ...."

"No. Don't 'but Homer' me. Between yesterday and today, it's too much and *not my job* to know where you are every minute."

"Of course not. I don't understand. I texted my three friends and told them I needed some time to myself. I was very upset about yesterday, and everyone was mad at me. And I felt they all needed to be responsible for their own actions. I needed some space.

"Plus," I pulled out the library documents, my notes, and the ship's roster, and stuffed them into Homer's hand, "It was about this. It was all because I was trying to do a good thing. And you, Homer, you of all people are yelling at me like this, when you should know me better. I'm not taking it!"

I ran back inside and opened the door to the stairway. I couldn't wait another moment to get away from Homer, and was not about to wait for the elevator.

Everything was wrong!

There must be something about me I don't understand that people will be so angry, rather than listen, or give a moment's pause to think things through. The thought crossed my mind to get back in the car and drive to Southern California to be with my parents. They were maybe mad at me now, too. I didn't even know if, in all of this unnecessary hullabaloo, my dad had been called.

Stopping at the fifth-floor landing to grab a breath of air as I'd run the whole way, I sat on a step and pondered my unpleasant fate. Weirdly,

I felt really sorry to have given Homer all that documentation, the only evidence I had of all my sleuthing. The only result of the appearances of the angel in the mirror.

"Well, really, it doesn't matter, Nikki," I said aloud. "They're all mad at you. No one cares about what you did. It's completely unimportant. Why the angel appeared, I have to now wonder, if this was meant to be the outcome. But going to be with your parents might really be the best thing. It's not right for Homer to feel as if he's my baby sitter. And it's not right about how I felt about *everything!*"

The thought seriously crossed my mind. I could go up, pack some things, and leave a note that I was going to stay with my parents. I could just get in the car and go.

Yikes! I barely know how to drive. Could I find my way to Laguna Beach from Seattle?

I could! That resolute Nikki, the Nikki who crawled on her hands and knees in the Underground City until she saw light, replied. I looked at my hand where I'd removed the ginormous sliver. It was red and swollen. And it hurt. I hadn't even noticed it, with all I'd been doing.

I stood. I needed to get some disinfectant on this wound, and I needed to sit quietly in my room, considering my options. Did I really want to be away from Mitch?

No.

But if he was really, truly angry with me like I'd never seen, as well as Homer angry with me like I'd never seen—who I'd have to see every day, and suffer his anger, or maybe even worse, his cold shoulder if I stayed—yeah. I could imagine not being here.

I dragged myself up the rest of the stairs and exited the stairwell on the seventh floor, then down the hall, letting myself into the apartment.

"Alone!" I said. "Thankfully. Now I …."

Yumi came out of the conservatory. "*Here you are!*"

"Oh! I thought you were with Alex and Mitch."

"No. I stayed here in case you showed up." An edge of accusation laced her delicate voice.

"Well, here I am," I said, feeling the overwhelming frustration and hurt welling up. "I'm here!"

"I don't understand why you've had to put everyone through all this. I …."

"Don't start with me, Yumi. I wanted some time to myself. It's not a crime. I did nothing wrong." I could feel my emotions rising, as the sting of Homer's anger washed over me again. "I don't deserve all of this … abuse. I don't deserve it, and I won't take it." I felt the whole miserable awfulness of everything wash over me.

"Mitch ranting at me, and then Homer ranting at me like I could never imagine he would talk to anyone, and now you!" I was up to shouting range now. "*No!* I won't take it!" I stomped down the hall to my room. "I'm going to go to Laguna Beach. I guess I'm just not old enough to take care of myself. I'm going to be with my parents!"

I slammed the door, and then as noisily as I could, threw the lock on the door. Flinging my backpack onto the bed, I stomped over to the windows and looked down, seeing nothing. I fumed and stomped back and forth across my room. The room with the mirror. The mirror that was the source of all my problems.

I couldn't help replaying Homer's words, his anger. How could he ever talk to me in that way? I stomped up and down, tears streaming down my face. I have never cried this hard since Grammy died. I'd felt impossibly lonely that day, and I felt the same way now. Everyone turned on me, and I was all alone.

As much as, right this moment, I wanted to simply be with my parents, I had to realize that they were probably mad at me too. I hadn't even scrolled through the messages and calls on my phone to see what kind of melodrama may have developed over my "disappearance," and I had no interest in looking at that now.

I finally sat on the edge of the bed, exhausted. I had to calm down, I had to sort my thoughts out. And, if I really intended to drive to Southern California, I had to pack and study a map.

I had to think about Homer for a minute. I had disappeared. And he *did* feel responsible for me. To the degree that he did, I wish he wouldn't, but he did. He wouldn't be Homer if he didn't really care about all the people he oversaw, coming and going from the building. And he'd implied that I had endangered his job. If this was true, he had reason to be afraid. And angry.

Not only that, but there was that time before when I had disappeared—it seemed so very long ago now. When I'd gone looking for Mitch. Although it seemed long ago to me now, it probably did not seem that way to Homer. It probably seemed to him like I was running off and disappearing all the time.

And then I thought about Mitch and Alex going so far as to drive to the underground city looking for me. I wished they hadn't, but, Nikki, I admonished myself, they only did it because they care about you. Because they love you.

Think it through!

Yes. All right, maybe everyone had responded like, well like, how else would they respond? And if I scared them, it only makes sense that there was a lot of emotion in their voices. Even though I wish they all could just have let me do what I had to do, in peace.

But I was still left with the thought that maybe I ought to be with my parents. Not awful, right? It was summertime, I'd get together with my old friends, go to the ocean, watch the surfers, and have a good time.

Yeah. Right. Just trying to think of no Mitch in my life made anxiety well up in me, worse than all the other anxieties rolled together. But then I thought, what if he's so mad at me, he wants to break up?

Ohhhh! this was not a good place to go. It was more than I could handle at this overwhelmed moment. That would absolutely decide it. If he said, "Nikki, we're through!" I would get in the car and drive, heading south.

Yumi tapped at the door. "Nikki!"

"Leave me alone, please. Just—for a while, leave me alone."

"Yes, but—I'm sorry, really, to bother you, but …."

Then I heard Homer. "Nikki, Homer here. Very sorry to invade your home, but I must talk with you."

"Homer, you made yourself profoundly clear. Really, I don't need to hear it again or some more. I don't." I knew I should make some sort of apology. But I didn't want to do it though a closed door, and I was in no mood to open the door. And, I *had* to decide if I was going to Laguna Beach, so I wasn't just shouting it out and about, when, really, I lacked the courage to do it.

"Nikki, I really must talk with you, please. Yumi says you said you were going to go be with your parents, and, if you truly are, I need to talk with you before you do."

"I haven't decided yet if I'm going to do that. I can't think right now. I'm all a muddle. I just tried to do a good thing, and everyone is furious with me. And it looks like I can't be responsible on my own, and I just … I just …. I don't know what I just. I just need to be left alone while I sort the madness that everyone knows as Nikki, out."

There was a soft chuckle from the other side of the door. "Not quite madness, dear girl. Won't you please let me in? I've looked at the papers you handed me. I … I really want to talk with you, face to face. Please."

Something in his voice broke me down. I unlocked the door, and Homer stepped into my room, looking incredibly uncomfortable. I saw Yumi in the hall, but I avoided eye contact as I closed the door again.

I turned to face Homer. "Yes?"

"Nikki, I wasn't wrong when I said your disappearing was causing me not only personal anxiety but endangered my job."

"I know, Homer. I've been thinking it through, and I realize the truth of that. I do apologize for causing you undue anxiety." I moved to the windows and looked down, watching the trees' branches sway in a breeze, which always calmed me. "But I do wish I could move about in my life without this relentless, constant, supervision.

"You know, it's been not quite a year since my family moved here. And last summer, when I felt like I was being torn from my whole life to move here—last summer before we moved here, and I was a whole year younger, I could go out alone and move about in my life without having to answer for my every move. My parents both worked, I'd be alone the entire day and not have to 'check in'—I really felt that texting my three friends that I needed to be alone, on the heels of all that noise from Mr. Zingas, because Alex didn't pay attention to the time, or whatever … oh, I just am tired of everyone being mad at me."

I turned to look at Homer, still standing by the door. Still looking incredibly uncomfortable. "Hmmm, I didn't know all that. You make some good points, Nikki. I only reacted to Mitch's concern that you had been gone all morning and were not answering your phone. My alarms went off.

"So, I apologize for talking to you the way I did. You've never seen me angry, it must have really surprised you."

"Shocked me. To my core."

"Well, I can get angry when I'm protecting the people I'm responsible for. I don't see myself as 'just the doorman' ...."

"I don't either, Homer," I interrupted.

"I see myself as the person who knows every, single resident in this building. Who knows a bit about each of their lives and a lot about their routines. I take pride in this ...."

"You should," I interrupted again.

"And when something threatens my position or maybe one of my charges...."

"You go off."

"I become concerned and involved."

"And then, you go off." I felt a tiny, little smile creep onto my face.

"Well, yes," Homer agreed soberly. "I guess I do go off. But it's rare, and takes a lot for me to ... 'go off.'" He sighed deeply. "But, now, can we set that aside?"

"Happily," I said.

I watched as he pulled the pages I'd recently stuffed into his hands from an inside pocket of his very tidy, double-breasted, taupe, brass-buttoned jacket. "These papers," he whispered, his voice full of emotion, "these documents, Nikki, how did you come by them?"

"I came by them by being absent all day. I'm not at liberty to say where the first document came from, that is Mitch's to tell or not. But I ended up in the main downtown library, and a delightful librarian, Elvira, pulled up the information about the family names and then, rather miraculously, I thought, found the article about the lost little boy, and she and I put the information together, so that you have your history, now, in your hands. And you can now …."

"I can now clarify some things with Mitch's mom."

"Yes." I heard commotion at the door as Mitch and Alex came into the apartment. I heard Mitch's voice raised to an unpleasant tone I'd never heard, although I could not make out his words, while at the same time, Yumi's soft voice appeared to be arguing with him. He began to storm down the hall, and I heard Yumi say, *Homer is there!*" Mitch became completely quiet.

Everyone became completely silent. Then I heard soft voices coming from the sofas in the living room.

I looked at Homer. "Mitch is mad at me too, you see. And he even knew a bit about what I was hoping to find out. I understand him being angry, because, like you, I guess I scared him, *even though* I texted him. I've never seen him this angry. Maybe he wants to break up with me. I'm too difficult. I'm too—I don't know, more than he wants to deal with."

"No, Nikki, no. My goodness, that boy is besotted with you."

"Besotted?" I had kind of an idea what the word meant, but I wasn't sure.

"Head over heels …."

"Head over heels? How … why do you say that?"

"Because I'm observant. He loves you, Nikki."

"I think it's possible to love someone and not be able to be with them. I read that on Instagram."

Homer laughed out loud. I don't think I've ever heard him laugh out loud. "And we know Instagram is the repository of all the world's wisdom."

Now he made me laugh, too. "It might be missing a few pieces. But this part I think is true, that you can love someone and not be with them. For whatever reasons."

"True. But not relevant in this case. Anyway, Nikki, thank you, thank you for this." He held the papers up.

"Well, the dressing down aside, you're welcome."

"And even that information about Relia's family name…."

"Yes. Like is on the cross-stitch sampler. I can't read it, so I never knew it was a name."

"And I've not paid much attention to it. I could have probably discovered a lot on my own, just researching that name."

"Well, now you don't have to. But, if you want to, you can go chat with Elvira. The Victorian era is her particular interest, and she's very nice."

"I'll do that! Won't that be interesting to learn more about my ancestors?"

"Yes," I said simply, thinking about the journal in my backpack, the actual, hand-written journal of his uncle and his charming life, all those years ago. I wanted to hand the journal to him this very minute. But I had to wait. It was Mitch's decision, and there was a lot revolving around it.

I couldn't give Homer the journal without telling him about the underground city, and I couldn't tell him about the underground city and not expect Mitch's mother to be told about it. It rapidly got complicated!

"Shall we join your friends?" Homer suggested. "They sound calmed down."

"Yes. Let's. But, first I need to know if you called my parents?"

"No, I didn't. I was about to, but I wanted to wait a bit longer. Quite frankly because I did have faith in you, that you were being responsible, that you would turn up. And that, as your text said, which Mitch showed me, you needed some time alone. But it's a good thing you turned up when you did because I was absolutely moments away from calling them."

"Thank you, Homer, for your belief in me. I hope my friends have had the same amount of faith in me."

We made our way down the hall to the living room, all three pairs of eyes of my friends glued on us. "Here I am, in the flesh, alive and well." I looked at my palm, which was really starting to throb. "Not entirely well. I have this wound I need to attend to."

Mitch jumped up. "What? What wound? You know, Nikki, I'm still mad at you, the scare you gave me when …" he glanced at Homer, "Well, you know when." He made a head gesture towards the door.

I followed his glance and saw my tool bag. "Yes. I know. I'm truly sorry, on one hand. But on the other, I do get to have some time to myself on the rare occasion. And speaking of the other hand, I need to attend to this." I held my beet-red hand up. "I got a sliver, a very big sliver, details pending until later. I'm pretty sure I got all of the sliver out, but I have to disinfect it. I'll be right back."

I went into the hall bathroom, but Mitch followed me, took my hand, and studied the sliver hole carefully. "I don't see any wood bits. How did this happen?"

"My flashlight and headlight gave out, and I had to crawl."

"*Ohhhh! Nikki*, how frightening!"

"I cannot lie, it was terrifying." I leaned into him, feeling contented and secure. "I imagined never being found. Which was the real fantasy, since you were there within hours. You and Alex must have passed me on the road."

"We must have." He put something that stung on my wound.

"Ouch!"

"You'll be all right," he said, wrapping a bandage on it.

"Yes. I will. I am. I … I thought, you were so angry, I thought maybe you would say you couldn't be with me anymore."

He turned me to face him and hugged me tightly. "No Nikki. Life would have no meaning. I'm afraid, sweet Nikki, that you're stuck with me. Yes, you can be a pile of surprises, sometimes. But it's all part of the package of the Nikki I love."

Granted, a small hall bathroom might not be the most romantic place to have this perfectly romantic interaction.

But, still, it was perfectly romantic.

I heard the doorbell ring. "Who could that possibly be?"

We stepped back into the hall just as Yumi let Mitch's mother in.

"Mom!" Mitch said, surprise in his voice. "What's up?"

"I was wondering if Nikki had been found, and I see she has. And Homer, who was so mad at her. Too mad at her! I told him not to be so angry. That she's a young adult, and knows what she's doing, and to leave her alone. Let her have her space."

"Wow!" I whispered. "Thank you!"

"You're welcome, dear. But why does everyone look like this? What's happening?"

"Homer was so angry with Nikki. And he sort of yelled at her …." Yumi said.

"Not 'sort of'—I really read her the riot act. And I was wrong. Just wrong. I've been eating crow and apologizing. Look at what she found out—just for me." Homer handed the papers to Relia. "She not only found out my ancestor's last name, which, of course, is my last name as well, but she discovered, by talking with a librarian, that your family name—different from mine, your family was on the same ship as my family."

Her brow furrowed as she studied the papers. "Is this about that thing you've told me about being related, and you were afraid to …."

"Yes," Homer said.

"You are such a … what is that thing I hear people call people when they're … oh, goofball. Homer, that's what you are, a silly goofball."

It was so incredibly funny, in her cute little accent. Yumi looked shocked, raising her eyebrows, while Mitch and I exchanged a look.

"Wow, Homer, I guess she told you!" Alex said.

We all broke out in giggles. Even, finally, Homer, who, at first, didn't seem to know how to take her insult. "But why do you say that?"

"All this tempest, just because you didn't want us to be—whatever that would be—tremendously removed cousins?"

"It bothered me," Homer said in his defense.

"It doesn't bother me!" Relia insisted. "Sometimes, my friend, you simply need to relax."

"I suppose you're right. But Relia, I don't want the young people to disrespect me, with you talking to me like this."

"We won't!" I protested. "We love and respect you."

My friends all joined in with enthusiastic agreement.

"Everyone, please excuse Mitch and me for a few minutes," I said. "I need to have a little chat with him—we'll be right back." Mitch joined me as I went down the hall into my room.

As soon as I closed the door, which I felt I needed to do because I didn't want certain people to hear what I was about to say, Mitch put his arms around me and whispered in my ear, "I'm really sorry for how I sounded, or even how I felt. The more I'm with you, the more I see how I need to simply trust you."

"I'm very glad to hear it," I said, releasing myself from his embrace—most reluctantly. "Because we have a big decision on our hands. And by we, I mean you." I sat on the bed and patted it for Mitch to come and sit by me, then I pulled the ancestor Homer's journal out of my backpack. "Look at this!" I turned to the back and opened the little empty pocket. "In here was the ship's roster that Homer's family was listed on. And, not only that, as Homer just said, also your mother's family."

"That is so amazing!"

"Yes. Isn't it? The librarian was an incredible source of information. She is a self-proclaimed Victorian expert, which claim she supported with a glut of information. She even reads a bit of Romanian, which made short work of her finding some of the papers I gave Homer a little while ago."

I handed the journal to Mitch and watched as he carefully turned the pages.

"Oh! Nikki!" he said softly. "What a dazzling discovery. How did you find this? Where was it?"

I pointed to my closet. "The mirror showed me. It was behind a little door in the wall of the dormer window, behind a darling Victorian watercolor."

Mitch could not pull his gaze from the lovely penmanship and the fascinating words of the long-ago Homer. "'Today the store is almost done,' 'I am now writing from my beautiful little desk,' 'Miss Sumner, the librarian, yes, I address her by name …' 'today the angel arrived!' Oh, Nikki, it is so touching. *Sooooo* touching. I want to read every word."

"I know. I did read every word. But you can see how it was that I ended up in the dark. I was completely in his world, up there in his little apartment, utterly forgetting that I was reading by flashlight. Until it started to flicker. There I was upstairs …."

Mitch shuddered. "What did you do, Nikki? I hate to think of you, all alone in that total darkness."

"I tied a rope to the tool bag and put it on the highest step I could reach, then tied the other end to my backpack. I super-carefully, took each step, stepping over the second from the top one. The door was unlocked, as you will recall, so I just stepped in and hauled up my tool bag. Which I didn't need.

"Of course, the scary part was going back down, when I didn't know if, at any moment, I would be plunged into total darkness, so I reversed my process quickly, hurried through the store out the front and onto the boardwalk, hoping against hope that my headlamp would stay lit until I reached natural light. But it gave out before then."

"Ohhh, no!" Mitch whispered.

"My thoughts, exactly. When would anyone find me? Then I got the idea that I could get down on all fours and crawl, one literal baby-step at a time until I came to light, which is what I did—and how I came by a two-inch sliver in my palm." I held my fingers apart, showing the length of the sliver.

"What am I going to do with you, Nikki?"

"I don't know. Love me?"

"Yes. Of course. Done."

"And otherwise, you need to take me as I am."

"I will. I'm learning to. But is it okay if I beg you to be careful?"

"I suppose," I said, feigning being aggrieved. "But getting to my subject, while we have a roomful of people wondering what we're up to in here, I feel that it's very important and, simply, the right thing to do to give this journal to Homer. I will never feel right as long as I have it and he doesn't."

"I see," Mitch quietly turned over what I said—and what it meant—for a few moments. "Yes, you're right, of course. But, if you give him this journal, he will insist on knowing how you came by it. And the only story that will suffice is the true story. And so we'll have to take Homer to the underground city. And we can't take Homer to the underground city without my mother."

"That neatly sums it up."

"And—you think we should do this?"

"Mitch, it's your decision to make. But, yes, I think it's going to be even more difficult to keep this truth from your mother, and, if Homer becomes … hmmmm, becomes your stepdad …."

"Oh, now, *there's* a thought."

"A *real* possibility, Mitch. Anyway, if he does, it'll be even more impossible to be gone for hours at a time when no one knows where we are."

"Then we must tell them." Mitch turned and looked out my long windows, contemplating. "I think it's all right. It'll be all right. Neither of them will tell anyone. And it'll make everyone's life easier, not having to keep the cover on it all the time."

I heaved a giant sigh of relief. "That's *exactly* what I hoped you'd say. No continuing to try and make up reasonable stories, which I'm not good at and not comfortable with."

"Let's do it."

"Right now?"

"Why not? Rip the bandage off. Everyone's assembled, no time, as they say, like the present."

"All right." Mitch handed me Homer's journal and we returned to the living room. There was the rumble of quiet conversation, but the conversations fell to silence as we came into the living room. "Mom, Homer, we have something to share with you. It's a pretty big something, and we're going to ask you to not share what we're about to tell you with anyone else."

"Oh!" Alex exclaimed. "You're going to tell them?"

"Yes," Mitch said. "Things have come to a head that we've decided this is the only practical choice."

I handed the journal to Homer. "I came upon this journal. It was written by your ancestor uncle that you mentioned to me." Puzzlement crossed his features as he took the journal from me. "The ship's roster that I handed you I found in the little envelope in the back of that journal."

He looked at the inside back cover, then back to the first page. He read in a very soft voice, "Dear Journal – today we begin our journey together. I guess most people write in a journal to recap their day, and whatever thoughts they have about that day. But this journal has only one purpose, and that's to record what I find out—and I do hope this journal has some significant entries—about my real family, and who I really am."

Homer gently turned to an interior page. He studied the entry with a small, quizzical frown between his brows. Then he read in a whispering voice, "You know, Journal, my affinity for angels, messengers of God, and comforters of the human family. I am sending a wire to order one in the morning. Even though a wire is expensive, I cannot wait! My angel is ten-feet tall and has an amazing face. I don't care about the expense of the marble angel, either, nor even the question Miss Sumner posed about where I'll put it."

He closed the journal and held it between his hands as if it was something sacred, "But,

Nikki, where did this come from? How did you get it?"

"That's what we're about share," I said. "And what we're asking that you keep secret. It's a pretty big secret, but I think you'll honor it for both Mitch's and Yumi's sake."

"Mitch and Yumi?" Mitch's mother exclaimed, confused.

"A long time ago," Mitch began, "I completely stumbled upon a magnificent find. And … Nikki, I don't feel quite comfortable trying to explain this right now."

"You'd rather just take them there?"

"Yes."

"It's too late to take you there today, but we'll do it tomorrow."

"Why not tell us now?" Homer asked.

"Because it will be more accurate—and awesome—if you see it for yourselves, without any less-than-complete chatter beforehand."

"I don't know who you are," Mitch's mother said, looking at him, mystification on her features.

"Sure you do, Mom. But tomorrow you'll know me better."

"I don't get off work until four," Homer said. "So it'll have to wait until then."

The four of us exchanged looks, and Mitch nodded. "Four p.m., everyone, in the parking lot, at my car."

Chapter XII

An Angel's Work is Never Done

The next day dragged by as if it knew the four of us were all on tenterhooks, although it was good because Mitch was able to go to his internship duties, and Alex spent some extra time helping his dad, trying to make up for the difficulty of two days before.

Yumi and I sat around, coming up with different potential scenarios that might happen when Mitch's mom and Homer were introduced to the underground city. We couldn't really guess what either one of them might say, or how they might feel.

It was all speculation, but it helped pass the time. Finally, it was four o'clock—Mitch called me from the parking lot. "I'm ready to go."

"We'll be right down. Are you calling Homer and your mom, too?"

"Yep. Right now. I wanted you two down here though for support."

"You don't need it, but we'll be right down. Bye." I looked at Yumi, "Let's go!"

We both slipped into our exploring shoes as we'd come to name them, pulled on our backpacks, and were soon on the elevator, riding silently down, wondering which of all of the scenarios we'd just spent time dreaming up was about to transpire.

We stepped outside. Alex stood by Mitch as they chatted quietly. "We're just considering the seating arrangement."

"What did you decide?"

"We have no idea. Should we put Mitch's mom in the front and Homer in the back, or the other way around, or any other way?"

"Let both of them ride in the back, and I'll ride in the back as well, and you and Yumi and Alex in the front."

"That works. I don't know why I was blocked."

"It's your *mother*, that's why."

"Speaking of … here she comes," Alex said, the only one of us facing the door.

"Hi, Mom," Mitch said.

"Hello, dear." She waved back toward the door. "Homer is coming, he's behind me."

"You can go ahead and get in the back."

"In the back?"

"Sure. So you and Homer can sit together. Nikki will sit back there with you, and Alex and Yumi up front with me."

"All right."

Right then, Homer, looking completely unfamiliar in jeans and a plaid shirt, came through the door.

"Hi, Homer. I see you're carrying a couple of flashlights. Fantastic!" Mitch observed.

"You can never go wrong with flashlights."

"True." Mitch gestured to the back seat. "Climb in the back, there, Homer, with Mom. The rest of us will pile in, and we'll be off."

And soon we were. I was surprised that Homer and Mitch's mom did not badger us at all about where we were going. I guess the two of them had a talk and decided to let us do with them as we would, as long as we showed them the mystery we promised to reveal.

Before long, the little hill came into sight, and Mitch pulled off the road, onto the knoll.

"Mitch," his mother protested, "what are you doing? This is private property."

"Yes," Yumi said. "And it belongs to my mother. It's all right."

"Is this true?"

"Of course it's true, Mom," Mitch answered. "Okay everyone, pile out. Get your backpacks." He went around to the back of the car and we grabbed our backpacks, and Mitch's and my tool bags, and headed for the dirt stairs. The four of us turned to see Mitch's mom and Homer standing, unmoved, staring at us.

"Come on, you two. "

"To where?" Homer asked.

In reply, the four of us, each in turn, started down the dirt steps. When we got to the bottom, we looked up, and finally, Homer and Mitch's mom peeked their heads over the edge.

"What!?" Mitch's mom cried. "What is this?"

"Just come down a few steps, Mom, so you can see, and I'll tell you."

Homer came down four steps and extended his hand up to Mitch's mom. She took it and stepped down to him slowly.

"Come on down the rest of the stairs."

His mother finally gathered courage and came down the rest of the stairs with Homer. "Where are we? What is this?"

"It's a far-away part of the underground city, when the city was rebuilt after the Great Fire. As this part of the city was at the very edge, it's in surprisingly good condition, and they just never built over the top of it here."

"It's incredible!" Homer exclaimed. "Relia, Mitch has really discovered something."

"I see that. I … just can't understand it," she answered, sounding mystified.

"You will understand it better over time. And we can come and explore more, some other time, too. But right now, the four of us would like to show you something even more amazing than what you're seeing right now. Shall we?"

"Yes," Homer said enthusiastically. "Let's! Come on, Relia."

"It's dark and scary," she answered.

We watched as Homer moved to her and put his arm around her. "I'll keep you safe, little kitten."

Awwww! I had to stifle saying it aloud, but it was so darn cute to see our Homer mushy and affectionate with our Mitch's mom.

"All right," she acquiesced. "I'll go for a little bit. But I get to come back when I want to."

"Of course!" we all agreed, while I thought, *hmmmm*, I'll have to be the one to bring her back while Mitch and Alex continue on.

Off we headed into the darkness, Mitch in the lead, then his mom, then Homer then Yumi, then me, then Alex. I was okay with all the lights and all the friends, but I couldn't help running some cold fear as our lights glinted off the darkness, recalling the terror I'd experienced when I lost my headlight, just the day before.

We moved past the first few houses, then Mitch stopped in front of Yumi's family's house. "This is where Yumi's ancestor aunt had a beautiful hat shop."

"Yes," Yumi said. "The display windows face the road that used to be on the opposite side of the houses."

"So your aunt knew my uncle?" Homer asked.

"For sure. Their businesses were near one another. I can't imagine that they would *not* have known each other."

"Small world."

"It is."

We walked on quietly, I was taking in landmarks as never before, given my experience of yesterday. There were some pretty interesting landmarks I came up with. Blue phosphorescence shaped sort of like a goldfish—or bluefish!—on the wall opposite the houses, a big creaking sound from the boardwalk at the house with no porch, etc.

"How are you doing, Mom?" Mitch asked.

"Better than I thought I would. I'm just so—awestruck."

"My feelings exactly, the first time I came down here." Mitch chuckled. "No. That's not right. That's how I feel every time I come down here."

"I can believe it," Homer interjected. "I think we're so quiet because we're dumbstruck and overwhelmed."

"Yes. Dumbstruck," Mitch's Mom agreed.

Before long, we came to the mercantile. It seemed the shortest trip there ever, in the wonderful community of friends.

Mitch stopped just beyond the path that led up the small incline to the mercantile. He gestured up to the front door. "This was your uncle Homer's store." He pointed up at the little dormer window. "And that's his apartment. All surprisingly intact. Shall we go?"

"Yes," Homer said, "of course. But, I'm feeling a bit overwhelmed. I read his whole journal last night, and now to see, with my own eyes, all the labor and love he poured into this building and his business, I … I'm overcome." He stepped on the little path and made his way up the hill to the front porch, where he stopped and watched Mitch's mom, and then the rest of us come up to join him.

"Lead the way, Mitch," he said.

"All right. I assume you left everything unlocked, Nikki, given that you were in a hurry to get to light."

"Yes. Everything unlocked. Not sure I would have locked anything, even without the 'no-light scare.' After all, no one's ever here but us."

"True." Mitch opened the door and tipped his invisible hat in such an impeccable imitation of Homer that it set us all to laughing, even Homer.

"Show off!" Homer said, stepping through the door.

"I have a good teacher!"

Relia stepped inside. "Oh, Homer, look at this lovely store." She wandered around, looking into the showcases. "Beautiful imported items. Practical items. Everything is here!" She turned to Yumi. "So—your mother owns the land, a by extension, this part of the underground city."

"Technically, I guess so," Yumi said, sounding uncomfortable. "But I don't feel like that at all. I mean, as far as I'm concerned—and I know my mother feels the same, everything in this store belongs to Homer. It's his inheritance. What do you think, Mitch?"

"I agree."

"Why are you asking Mitch what he thinks?"

"Because my mother has appointed him overseer of the underground city, and, although he doesn't actively come into the position for a while, I want to run everything by him, so that when he does take over, it's according to what he thinks best."

"Yumi's mother appointed my son as overseer of this property," Relia said, soft and mystified.

"Well, yes. Because he's the one who discovered it. He loves it and he'll take the best care of it. And, as I say, the contents of the mercantile belong to Homer, to use or leave, as he pleases."

"In which case," Homer said, "in return for my profound thanks for helping fulfill my heart's desire, I invite you to take something that will remind you of this day when you all were so kind and loving to your Homer."

There wasn't anything I felt compelled to take from the mercantile. Seeing everything in situ warmed my heart. But I knew Yumi so wanted that one particular chatelaine for her art. I looked around for her, and, yes, there she was, standing over the case, looking at that very item.

I caught Homer's eye and gestured toward Yumi.

He went to stand by her and followed her gaze to the item within. "Oh, that is so beautiful!" he said softly. "I see it has a little notepad and a pen—just the sort of thing a young artist needs!" He reached to open the case, and with only a small whine, it slid open. He took out the beautiful chatelaine and handed it to Yumi. "Here, my dear put this gorgeous item to some good, practical use!"

"Oh! Really, Homer, really?"

"Absolutely really!"

Holding the silver chains close, she gave him a big hug. "Thank you, Homer. I must tell you that

I have thought and thought and thought about this beautiful item since I first saw it. I've not been able to get it out of my mind. But are you really certain, Homer? Maybe it should stay here, with everything else, like a museum."

"No, Yumi. My uncle intended to provide goods to be used. If he were here right now, I know he would be as happy as I am that this beautiful silver work of art be out in the world, used, appreciated, and loved." He turned to me. "What about you, Nikki? What's your favorite thing in the mercantile."

Mitch chuckled, guessing what I was likely to say.

"My very favorite thing in the mercantile cannot be moved. But I wouldn't have it any other way."

"What would that be?"

"Follow me." I took Homer, and the whole group, through to the storage room, then stopped in front of the angel.

"*Ohhhh! My!*" Homer exclaimed. "*The angel!*"

"Yes. The angel. So—you can see how perfect he is right here—overseeing the underground city."

"Yes. Oh, I'm so glad that I got to see this magnificent work of art, most likely carved by a relative, long, long, ago."

"Gorgeous!" Mitch's mom whispered.

We meditated on the angel for a few more moments, and then I led Homer out the little back door, to flash the light on the stairs, as everyone came out behind us. "We don't know how safe the stairs are. Yumi and I have successfully gone up and down, stepping over the second step from the top because it feels wobbly."

"But I wouldn't trust it to hold Mitch or Homer or me," Alex said. "If you really want to see the apartment, the ladder is against the wall, if you can climb a ladder, Homer."

"I have indeed, climbed many a ladder, but is there anything up there in particular to see?"

"Well, there's the clever place I found the journal, and there's an adorable watercolor that hid the secret door, that you might enjoy seeing."

All right. Ladder it is." Homer moved to the ladder, climbed it in moments, and soon stood on the stair landing. He held onto the pipe railing, stepped lightly on the landing, then through the door into the little, cozy, apartment.

"I want to be there with him," I said, and scurried up the stairs before anyone could argue with me. Inside the apartment, Homer stood in the middle of the living room, stunned.

"Over here," I moved to the little dormer window. "I didn't even put things back together. I'd been so engrossed in reading the journal, I forgot where I was, and forgot that my batteries would wear down.

"But, anyway, Homer, look here at this clever little door in the wall. This is where I found the journal. There was this sweet watercolor over it."

Homer studied the little door, then shut it and hung the painting on its hook. "But, Nikki, what made you even consider looking here?"

"That, for the moment, must remain my secret."

"All right. I'm grateful for your secret, whatever it is." He shined his light on the painting, giving it a good study. "Well, this is a darling watercolor, this little boy watching the puppy cloud go by. Did you see that?"

"I sure did, Homer."

"I think I'll take it with me."

"I think you should! We'll put it in Mitch's backpack, it's bigger than mine."

Homer handed me the painting and then wandered around the apartment. "I can really feel his presence."

"Yes? What's it like?"

"It's like … family."

"Lovely."

"I can come back again, can't I?"

"Of course, Homer. You're now a member of *The Secret Underground City Society.*

"There's such a thing?"

"Just now, this very moment."

Homer laughed. "I'm a founding member, then."

"Indeed."

He took another turn around the apartment, then turned to me, smiling the sweetest smile I'd ever seen our sweet Homer smile. "Let's go."

We stepped out, I reached the painting down to Mitch. "Will that fit in your backpack without getting damaged?"

He opened his backpack and carefully wound a towel around the painting, and then slid it into his backpack. By the time he had that done, Homer was on the ground, and I was still at the top of the stairs. I turned and closed the door, and made my way down the stairs, holding onto the rail, with plenty of people below, ready to catch me.

Unhappily, Mitch did not grab me off the second step like before. Well, his mother was standing right there, which might have had something to do with it.

Our two new initiates decided they'd had enough exploring for the day. It was time to head home.

Chapter XIII

A Bit of Ceremony

A few days later, Yumi, Alex, and I were invited to Mitch's for, we were told, a "thank you" dinner. As far as I was concerned, with his mother's incredible cooking and baking skills, the thanks would all be on our side.

Mitch led the three of us into the dining room, where Homer was fussing with arranging dishes on the table. Mitch's mom came in, with a gigantic salad bowl. "Hi, kids, make yourself at home!"

As she left, Mitch and Homer followed her, and soon the table was laden with dishes of delicacies, their various and amazing aromas vying for our attention.

"Sit, everyone, let's eat. No need for ceremony!" Relia said.

We all sat, except for Homer. "Yes, there's a need for a bit of ceremony," he said. "Yesterday I asked Alex if he would help me with something, and, of course, he did. I wanted it to be a surprise. I saw a particular item when we were in the mercantile, and Alex and I retrieved it yesterday."

He came to the opposite end of the table to stand stood by Relia. Bending over her, he took her hand. "It's far too soon for the larger question, but, before these charming witnesses who are instrumental in changing my life, would you, dear Relia, be willing to enter into in a committed friendship with me, with the possibility of it becoming more meaningful over time?"

Relia stood. "Of course, you funny and strange man. Of course. Have I ever known anyone as sweet and giving as you? No. I know this is not easy for you, and, as you say, before these charming witnesses, but, yes, let us agree that we have something that has the potential of blossoming into something beautiful between us."

Homer pulled a small box from his pocket. "As I say, I saw this in the mercantile when we were down there, and, well, I knew it belonged to you." He opened the box and revealed a gorgeous, large, rectangle cut, sparkling blue sapphire.

"*Oh, Homer!*" Mitch's mom whispered.

He took the ring out of the box and slipped it on her finger.

"Kiss her!" Alex said.

"Yes," Yumi and I chimed in, "Give her a kiss."

Mitch kept silent, but I guessed by the massive grin he had on his face, he was happy, as our beloved doorman gave his mother a rather chaste and gentle kiss.

* *

Later that night, after we'd all eaten more than we could imagine possible, after the "good-nights" were said among us, Mitch walked me to my door and kissed me long and sweetly.

"You've done an incredibly good deed, Nikki."

"I'm glad you feel that way."

"I've never seen such a beautiful, relaxed, smile on my mother, in my entire life. She deserves to be happy."

"She does indeed."

He leaned down and kissed me again. "Good-night, my darling fairy-dust magician."

I chuckled as I let myself into the apartment and down the hall to my room. I had a feeling that someone was waiting for me.

I went into my closet. After a few moments, as my eyes adjusted to the darkness, the angel manifested slowly in the mirror. He grew and grew, until he took up the whole mirror, in his brilliant, other-worldly light. I wanted to step back, but there was no place to step back to.

His intimidating marble features softened for once, as he looked at me. His unbelievable eyes! They shifted from stone-cold white to an astonishing color that is not in earth's rainbow. He made a small nod, then faded from view.

THE END

Nikki loved having you join her in
The Angel in the Ṁirror

Did you red the first book in Nikki's Adventures
in *The City Under Seattle*?
In case you missed it, here's the first few pages
of:

The People in the Ṁirror

Chapter 1
Gargoyle Faces

Peered I up into the drizzly sky at the tall, sad, gray front of the apartment building. rising up into a sad, gray sky, and I thought ... I cannot believe I have to call this place home.

An irritating mist-rain-wetness fell into my eyes as I made out gargoyle faces halfway up the building. I looked farther up and saw wet, gray gargoyle bodies at the top of the building—up there in the shifting mists. So a person could tell where the gray building stopped and the gray sky took over, I guessed.

"Isn't it fabulous?" Dad asked, all cheery like he'd built the building himself and was really proud of his work. He moved the umbrella he was sort of holding over Mom and me around some more, shaking more water on us than if there was no umbrella.

"It's ... really something," Mom said.

Good. At least she doesn't think it's "fabulous."

For some reason we continued to stand there, drinking in the view, I guess, Dad still beaming.

"Kind of shades of Rosemary's Baby though—don't you think?" Mom finally ventured.

"Nah!" Dad said, "Not at all! Wait 'til you see the inside, it just doesn't quit."

Oh boy, I thought, more and more of this. "Well, let's go see it then," I said, trying to resign myself to two things: one; I was actually going to have to live in an apartment building that two; came from some old horror movie.

"Good idea," Mom agreed. "Let's go inside, we're getting wet."

"Oh! Sorry!" Dad, all apologetic moved the umbrella around some more, which made sure we were good and wet. "Well, okay," he said behind us. Mom and I had made a beeline for the front door.

At the door stood a "portly" doorman, tall and round, wearing a dark taupe uniform. Yeah. Taupe. That color that just ... isn't really gray, isn't quite brown. He held the door open for us. Felt pretty weird. I can open doors myself, thank you very much.

"Welcome, Mr. Francis!" The doorman said in a reserved jolly way. "This must be your lovely family."

"Right, Homer. My wife, Clarice and my daughter, Dominique, but we usually call her Nikki. Clarice, Nikki, our doorman, Homer."

I couldn't believe it, he actually tipped his hat. No one had ever done that to me. But then, I'd never been introduced to a doorman before.

Once inside, I saw another man in a different sort—but same color—uniform, on the phone, so Dad didn't introduce us, thank goodness. But I could just feel him memorizing Mom and me as he nodded to Dad.

"Security guard," Dad whispered as we passed him.

Why whisper? I wondered. We weren't doing anything wrong.

We stopped in front of elevator doors that were all shiny silver and brass, with artistic designs on them like Art Deco, which, actually, I like. Okay. So the elevator doors I can live with. Dad pushed the button and one of the elevator doors slid open. Then Dad pushed "7" once we were inside.

"Well...." I said after the doors slid shut and I gently shook the rain from my hair with my fingertips, "I just wonder what all the paranoia's about."

Mom and Dad turned and looked at me as if I'd just learned to speak, for pity's sake. They both looked completely bemused.

"What do you mean?" Dad finally asked.

"Those men checking us out, seeing if we have a right to be here."

Neither of them said anything as the elevator door slid open. Dad led us down the hall to "717." The carpet in the hall was so thick I felt like I was sinking in it up to my ankles. It had a heavy, scrolly, burgundy and gray Victorian print. Then I noticed the soft gray walls and the ornate, brass wall sconces every few feet that had these little pink bulbs in them. I had to admit, silently, of course, that the whole effect gave the hall a cozy, warm light.

So, all right, nice elevator doors, nice light in the hall. Not much to go on, but better than nothing.

Dad waited until he let us in the apartment before he answered me.

"It's security, Nikki, not paranoia. They're there for our protection."

"Yeah, well," the irritation I felt when the "security guard" checked me out rose up my throat again, "no more casually having a bunch of friends over after school, huh?"

Dad studied me for a moment, a little frown working its way across his forehead like happens when he has to sort out something new. "I hadn't thought about that, sweetheart. But it'll all work out."

I nodded, thinking, I'm sure my friends—of course, I don't have any friends here, so it's completely moot—but, anyway, I'm sure if I *had* any friends, they'd all just love to come into a stuffy place like this.

But I kept my mouth shut. Another thought kept to myself. Dad can't help it he got transferred to Seattle. Just because I'm not happy I don't suppose I have to go out of my way to make him feel miserable.

Anyway, I finally looked around the apartment, and my jaw hit the floor—metaphorically. The place was beautiful! Walls a pale peach, with solid cherry woodwork in the door and window frames—I took shop last semester and had gotten into learning about different types of wood, and knew you didn't see cherry woodwork that often.

Dad had subleased the apartment from a man in his company who'd been sent to England for a year, so the place was completely furnished. All the furniture was big, solid antiques, mostly made of deep rich walnut, with a couple of cherry end tables. I liked it all on sight. Thank goodness the people hadn't gone in for all that spindly Louis-the-Whatsit stuff!

We went from the foyer into a huge living room, where Mom stopped in her tracks. She quietly breathed, "Wow!" An actual baby grand piano took up the entire corner. And it *was* "wow." I knew this made Mom happy. She'd told us both that she was going to get back to her piano playing if Dad dragged her away from teaching third grade for a year. Mom loved those kids.

The baby grand must be the "little surprise" Dad had been hinting and hinting at for the last couple weeks after he came back from Seattle from signing the lease on the apartment. Mom went straight to the piano, sat down and played a couple scales. The sound swelled in fat round notes right to the walls.

"Beautiful quality," she said, "and doesn't even need to be tuned."

We toured the rest of the apartment. Three bedrooms, two with private baths, a kitchen, a little breakfast nook, a formal dining room, and an actual greenhouse room on the corner of the building with two exterior glass walls, full of a riot of all kinds of plants. The whole place was like out of a Victorian movie. I hated to have to admit it, but it was altogether pretty cool.

"Didn't I tell you?" Dad got just more and more proud of himself as Mom "oohed" and "ahhed" at everything, and I even let out a couple of "oohs." It was that impressive. We came back to the living room and settled on facing sofas, covered in a soft, pale green and peach scrolly-patterned velvet.

"This isn't an apartment," I finally said. "It's a house, stuck up in a building. I think it's bigger than our house."

"I told you it was huge," Dad said.

"You said it was a huge *apartment*. I didn't know apartments could be bigger than a house."

"You're not in Laguna Beach anymore."

"Yeah, Dad. I got that part," I shrugged, my depression returning. No. I was not at home. I was not with my friends. I was not going to hang out at the beach today. Or any day soon. I was not going to school on Monday at the school I pretended to hate, but now missed in a mega way. No movies with friends tonight. No shopping tomorrow.

Yes. That old depression climbed right out of that gray sky and poured itself into me.

Chapter 11
Movement in the Mirror

But then I pulled myself together somewhat, and tried to be philosophical. I thought, a few days later, about how there was bad and good in most things. This was something my grandmother told me when I was only three or four and I'd accidentally left my treasured picture book she'd given me at the playground—Tootles Favorite, Funny Friends. When we went back to get it, it was gone. I cried so hard I started hiccoughing. That's the first time my grandmother said to me, "There's bad and good in most things."

About a week after that Mom handed me a package and said, "This came for you in the mail." I tore it open and there I held in my hands, *Tootles Favorite, Funny Friends!* I thought at the time it was magic, but now I guess my grandmother got another copy and sent it to me.

Anyway, back to now and about living in this apartment. On the bad side was the security guard, but Homer, the doorman, had gone over to the good side just because he turned out to be such a nice guy. He talks to me like I'm a person, not a kid, which is excellent. On both the good side and the bad side was the new school. Good—only three blocks from home. Bad—after four days, no one has even said "hi" to me. Another bad—the non-stop drizzling sky. I always felt wet. And cold.

Very definitely good—my room. As big as our living room at home, with a gigantic private bathroom the size of my entire bedroom at home.

And, as I'm not entirely heartless and selfish, also on the good side—how much Dad loved his job here, which I know because practically every day he's said, "I love my job here!" and how much Mom loved that baby grand piano. As I made up my "THE APARTMENT AND SEATTLE: GOOD–BAD" lists she was playing Beethoven's Fifth. It floated on the air like sweet whipped butter.

I wished I had something I loved so much I could completely lose myself in it. The only thing I loved like Dad loved his work and Mom loved playing the piano was reading—but that's not a talent, it's a hobby. You couldn't make more of reading than just ... reading. I was reading the "Horror in the Heights" series. The heroine in the pictures on the cover of the books looked exactly like I wished I looked.

I put down the *"Horror in the Heights, #6— Working with Goblins, Pixies and Gnomes"* I was reading and got up to study myself in the mirror inside the walk-in closet. This closet was the other incredibly great part about my room, huge! closet. A room all by itself. It was next to my bathroom, and pretty much the same size as the bathroom, with a gigantous mirror on the back wall, big enough for me to practice ballet in front of it—if I took ballet.

But it was the strangest mirror I'd ever seen, with a dark, smoky quality. I decided it was all dark and smoky because it was so old. Whatever the reason, I loved the way it made me look. Why? Because everyone always says I'm "cute" and I hate being called "cute." There's nothing special about "cute."

But the dark, smoky mirror faded my freckles, and made my pale blue eyes a shade darker, which looked so exotic. Everyone in my family has pale eyes, and it just seemed to me that people with dark eyes came from exciting places. The mirror made my hair a shade darker too. Now, finally, it had a color I could name besides "dishwater blonde." What kind of a color is "dishwater blonde" anyway? Ugh!

Mom and Dad had forbidden me to "put any permanent chemistry" on my hair "for the time being," whatever that meant—because Mom had read some article about how hair color damaged your brain, or something. That didn't mean I didn't fantasize about having hair that was lighter or darker. The mirror clinched it—I'd definitely go darker!

"Enough primping, your highness," I told my reflection. "Time to get at your homework." Since nothing else was going on in my life, I might as well get good grades. Look to the future, Dad always said. Yeah, especially when nothing was happening in the present.

But—and here's where the weird stuff began—just as I turned from the mirror, I saw something move in it.

I turned back to the mirror and peered into it ....

Then I shrieked and jumped. There was a man and a woman in the mirror, talking to each other in a faded light....

Thank You ....

For reading Nikki's story, **The Angel in the Mirror**.

Nikki has continuing adventures in **The People in the Mirror and Millie in the Mirror**, where she, Mitch, Yumi, and Alex continue to explore Seattle's mysterious *Underground City*.

Is there a story you'd like to read about Nikki's adventures? We'd love to hear about it!

If you've enjoyed Nikki's story, we hope you'll tell your friends – and tell us, too!

Until Next Time,

Thea Thomas
&
Blythe Ayne

About Thea ....

I live in the greater Portland, Oregon area. I love the Great Northwest where the rainy weather, lush green territory, waterfalls, mountains, charming neighborhoods, the Pacific ocean nearby, and a strong writing community—all contributing to making my writing life a dream come true.

You can write to me at:

Thea@EmersonandTilman.com

Have a Happy Day!
Thea

I live in a forest with a few domestic and numerous wild creatures, where I create an ever-growing inventory of books and short stories, with a bit of wood carving when I need a change of pace.

All the creatures in my forest and I are glad you "stopped by." If you enjoyed **Millie in the Mirror,** I hope you'll share it with others.

If you'd like to write me, I'd be happy to hear from you!

Blythe@BlytheAyne.com

www.BlytheAyne.com

'Til We Meet Again!
Blythe